"It's quieted down," Eunice commented

Really, those battles of their neighbors, the Powells, were always so much more entertaining than TV soaps. "Of course!" She brightened. "Lucy and Mike may have decided to kiss and make up."

"You're such a romantic, my dear," Clara, her longtime friend, said. "My guess is they've knocked each other unconscious."

Eunice tsked. "I may be a romantic, but you're definitely a cynic, Clara. Those two may have their rows every now and then . . ."

"Every now and then? They've lived in our apartment building nearly eight months and I don't think they've ever gone more than two days before there's been a blowup."

"Yes. Still, you only have to look at them to know they're wildly in love with each other," Eunice insisted.

"You may call it love, Eunice," Clara replied sharply. "I call it warfare."

Eunice giggled. "Well, dear. As the saying goes, all's fair in love and war."

Elise Title has always been intrigued by couples who are total opposites. In *Just the Way You Are,* Elise takes two very different personality types and has them tie the knot. Then, as so often happens in real life, her heroine Lucy Warner and hero Mike Powell soon decide that they want their mate to be more like themselves—forgetting that it was their very differences that drew them together. Elise had a lot of fun writing her madcap romance and hopes that readers have as much fun reading about the trials and tribulations of Lucy and Mike...and their "siblings"!

Books by Elise Title

HARLEQUIN TEMPTATION
358—JACK AND JILL
412—ADAM & EVE
416—FOR THE LOVE OF PETE
420—TRUE LOVE
424—TAYLOR MADE

Don't miss any of our special offers. Write to us at the following address for information on our newest releases.

Harlequin Reader Service
P.O. Box 1397, Buffalo, NY 14240
Canadian address: P.O. Box 603,
Fort Erie, Ont. L2A 5X3

JUST THE WAY YOU ARE

ELISE TITLE

Harlequin Books

TORONTO • NEW YORK • LONDON
AMSTERDAM • PARIS • SYDNEY • HAMBURG
STOCKHOLM • ATHENS • TOKYO • MILAN
MADRID • WARSAW • BUDAPEST • AUCKLAND

Published April 1993

ISBN 0-373-25538-1

JUST THE WAY YOU ARE

Prologue

LUCY WARNER POWELL gave her husband, Mike, an indignant look. "I'm self-involved? Extravagant? You have the gall—"

"Gall? It doesn't take gall, Lucy. It's as plain as the nose on your face. And speaking of your nose . . ."

Lucy edged her nose right up to Mike's, which took some doing, considering he was six-one and she was five-eight. She had to stand on her tippy toes. Well, at least all those ballet lessons as a kid were finally paying off.

"What about my nose?" She narrowed her catlike green eyes, settled one hand on her slender hip, curved the other into a no-nonsense fist, and gave her husband one of her infamous I-dare-you looks.

Mike Powell knew that look only to well. He'd seen it often enough in the eight tumultuous months he and Lucy had been married. He was also pretty familiar with that right hook of hers. Fortunately it usually missed its target. And they said redheads had tempers! This was one blonde who put all those carrot tops to shame.

"What about your nose?" he tossed back. "I'll tell you about your nose. Your nose veers to the right, that's what."

His hand caught her wrist just as she started to swing. "Oh, no, you liar." She hissed, trying to wrench her hand free. "It does not veer. It has never veered. My nose is perfectly straight. Not to mention that this nose that you seem to find such fault with just happens to have graced over a dozen magazine covers in its day."

He gave her one of his infamous crooked grins. "You said it yourself. 'In its day.'"

Two bright red spots flared on Lucy's high-sculpted cheekbones. "Oh, I hate you, Michael Powell. I'll have you know I could still grab a cover away from any of my models if I wanted it. But, I happen to like running the show instead of being run ragged. And—and furthermore, you always said you loved my nose."

"All I'm saying is that it veers to the right. If that hurts your cover-girl vanity, well, that's too damn bad. Furthermore, don't you think it's a little...neurotic to feel you have to have perfect looks?"

Now that was hitting a bit below the belt. What model— present or past—didn't have a degree of vanity? It went with the territory.

He was about to apologize when Lucy finally managed to wrench her hand free from his grasp. "I don't know why I ever married you," she snapped. "I must have been out of my mind. You're nothing but an uptight, pompous, smug stuffed shirt—"

"You're nothing but a spoiled brat," he countered, forgetting all about the apology.

"Oh-oh." Lucy grabbed Mike's breakfast plate from the nearby patio table. He ducked just in the nick of time and the plate went sailing over the balcony railing.

The Terrace of Apartment 1432C

"OH, LOOK AT THAT PLATE. Isn't that the same china pattern as you bought for your granddaughter Cynthia?" Eunice

Blanford, a diminutive white-haired woman in her early seventies, nonchalantly asked her friend, Clara.

"I'm not sure. It went by so quickly. Pity if it is. Costs a pretty fortune," Clara Ponds replied airily, pouring the morning tea for herself and her companion.

Eunice added two sugars to her cup and took a sip. "What did he say about soiled hats?"

Clara, a large, buxom woman a couple of years Eunice's senior, who was forever watching her waistline, opted for only one sugar cube. "No, dear. That was spoiled brat. He called her a spoiled brat."

"Well, that isn't a very nice thing for him to say," Eunice declared, biting into her buttered scone, then genteelly dabbing the crumbs from her lips with a linen napkin.

"No, I quite agree. It wasn't nice," Clara replied, eyeing her companion's scone with envy. "But then, she did call him pompous. And a stuffed shirt."

Eunice shrugged. "My Oliver was a bit of a stuffed shirt. Not that I would ever have dreamed of saying as much to his face, may he rest in peace."

Clara broke down and snatched up the one remaining scone from the bread basket in the center of the table. "Young couples today have no manners. Why, they just say anything that comes into their heads. I really think that's why..." The sentence trailed off as Clara and Eunice both watched another piece of fine bone china sail by them. This time it was a coffee cup.

"I do think it is the same pattern," Eunice said.

"Yes, dear. I believe you're right," Clara mused, adding just a tad of strawberry jam to her buttered scone.

The Terrace of Apartment 1532C

"... EXACTLY WHAT I MEAN," Mike shouted after the cup went

whizzing by his right ear. "It doesn't faze you in the least that you've just chucked a good fifty dollars or more over the balcony. It's just another example of your utter disregard for money, your irresponsible—"

"I didn't mean to chuck it over the balcony!" Lucy shouted back. "I meant to hit you. And it would have been worth it at double the price."

"Oh, that's very mature, Lucy. Very mature."

"At least I can express myself. I'm not the one who's tied up in knots, always worried about letting loose. Look at you. Look at your tie."

"What's wrong with my tie?" he demanded.

"It's hideously drab. But that's beside the point," Lucy said insouciantly. "The point is, you always pull your tie so tight around your collar, it's a wonder it doesn't cut off your circulation. Or maybe it does. Maybe that's part of your problem."

"I don't have a problem. And this tie is not drab. It's . . . tasteful and restrained. Besides what do *you* know about restraint? If it isn't purple and orange, with wild flowers . . ."

Lucy pushed back her thick mane of glowing, honey-blond hair from her face. "I detest orange. If you knew anything about me at all, you'd know that. And if you're trying to imply that I have cheap taste . . ."

"Cheap? No, darling. That's one adjective I'd never use where you're concerned. Gaudy, flamboyant, frivolous? Yes, yes, yes. Cheap? Never."

Lucy gave Mike a frozen stare. "Well, one cheapskate in the family is already one too many, thank you."

He glared back at her. "Oh, it is, is it? There is a solution to *that* problem, you know."

They eyed each other in stony silence.

The Terrace of Apartment 1432C

"IT'S QUIETED DOWN," Eunice commented, a shade of disappointment in her voice. Really, the battles of the Powells were always so much more entertaining than those television soaps. "Of course—" she brightened "—they may have decided to kiss and make up."

Clara slipped a shortbread cookie into her mouth, deciding to diet seriously tomorrow. "You're such a romantic, my dear. My guess is they've knocked each other unconscious."

Eunice tsked. "I may be a romantic, but you are a cynic, Clara Ponds. Those two may have their rows every now and then—"

"Every now and then? They've lived here nearly eight months and I don't think they've ever gone more than two days—maybe three on the rarest occasion—before there's been a blowup."

"Still, you have only to look at them to know they're wildly in love with each other," Eunice insisted.

"You may call it love, Eunice," Clara said, reaching for a second cookie. "I call it warfare."

Eunice giggled. "Well, dear. As the saying goes, all's fair in love and war."

The Terrace of Apartment 1532C

"IT IS HOPELESS, isn't it?" Lucy said quietly, the fight and the emotional strain of it all having exhausted her.

"My tie or your nose?" He could see his weak attempt at humor wasn't going to work.

"I can't go on like this, Mike," she said, walking to the terrace railing. She looked out at the Manhattan summer skyline and then down into the empty street, hoping no one had gotten beaned by one of those pieces of fine bone china she'd sent flying. "These fights are wearing me out."

Mike frowned, staring off into space. "Finally. Something we agree on."

She spun around to face him. "It was a mistake from the start. We should have both known better."

He smiled ruefully. "We did know better. We just chose to ignore what we knew."

"We can't go on ignoring it, though, can we?"

Mike's smile was replaced by a frown. "No. You're right. We can't."

They stared intently at each other. Lucy surveyed her husband. She saw a tall, slender, very handsome young man in a tailored, conservative blue suit and spit-polished black leather shoes, his dark hair razor-cut short. He looked every bit the astute, successful accountant that he was. His tie, she conceded but wasn't about to admit aloud, really wasn't all that drab.

And what did Mike see as he looked at Lucy? A long-limbed beauty whose face had every business gracing dozens of fashion-magazine covers over the years. And if her nose did veer ever so slightly to the right, it only added to her astonishing looks, giving her face a special uniqueness. Lucy was one of a kind. Not that he'd ever tell her what he was thinking at this juncture.

"So," Mike said awkwardly, rubbing his hands together, then shoving them into the pockets of his jacket. "I guess..."

Lucy's gaze skidded off her husband's face. "Yes, I...guess so."

"That is . . ."

Lucy's eyes zeroed back in on Mike. "That is?" She couldn't completely mask the touch of eagerness in her voice.

Mike loosened his tie a fraction, then immediately tightened it. "You could...make some changes, Lucy. Learn to be a bit more responsible, organized, less extravagant . . ."

"*I* could make some changes? *I?*" she said indignantly. "You have the nerve, the audacity . . ."

He scowled. "Forget it. You couldn't change if your life depended on it."

"Oh, and I suppose you could," she challenged.

"If there was some reason to change, I certainly could," he countered.

"Oh, I see. You think it's perfectly fine to be rigid, supercilious, patronizing and a cheapskate to boot."

"This is what I get for trying to offer you some constructive criticism, Lucy. You just deflect it and toss it back in my face."

"Is that what I do? Well, maybe I'm not making my point clear enough."

Before Mike knew what was happening, Lucy had managed to grab up her breakfast plate, this one with plenty of scrambled egg left on it.

"Lucy—"

She didn't miss her target this time, but pushed the plate smack dab into her husband's face.

When she released her hand, the plate crashed to the terrace floor and shattered. One more piece of fine bone china bit the dust. Little drippings of egg rolled down Mike's cheeks, which were a lot redder than usual, and down the front of his ever-so-recently-immaculate navy summer jacket.

Lucy took one look at her husband and realized she might have gone a step too far this time. She began to edge around the table toward the patio door that led into the apartment. "Now, Mike . . ."

Mike began to circle the table after her, the redness gone completely from his cheeks. Save for the smattering of yellow egg that remained, his complexion was ash white.

"Don't do anything you'll regret now, Mike." She darted for the open patio door.

But Mike was too fast for her. Catching hold of her wrist with one hand, he swiped up the china jam pot from the table with the other.

"Mike. Mike, you wouldn't. You wouldn't, Mike. It's...it's beneath you—"

The Terrace of Apartment 1432C

EUNICE WAS gathering up the breakfast dishes. "I still say those two were meant for each other. Anyway, Clara, what about that saying, 'Opposites attract'? You have to admit that's the case with the Powells."

"Oh, they attract, all right," Clara agreed. "It's what happens between them afterward that's the problem."

Eunice tilted her head up as she heard a high-pitched feminine squeal from the terrace above. "I bet he's pulling her into his arms this very minute. . . ."

The Terrace of Apartment 1532C

STRAWBERRY JAM drizzled down Lucy's wavy hair and down her face, as well. She stood very still, as did Mike.

"Go on. Say it, Lucy. That was very childish of me." He cleared his throat and meticulously picked little pieces of egg off his jacket. "Not that your move was particularly adult."

He saw that she hadn't moved a muscle. The jam was starting to drip onto the white collar of her dress. "Lucy..."

"No, Mike. Don't..."

They stared at each other, a protracted leaden silence following.

Lucy's gaze dropped, following the trail of strawberry jam that was now running down the front of her exotic jungle-print jersey dress. Very slowly, she raised her eyes back to her husband's face.

"I want a divorce, Mike." Even as she heard herself saying the words, she couldn't believe her ears. How absolutely awful, she thought despairingly, to love a man she hated.

Mike's stomach muscles constricted. He felt as if Lucy had landed one of her right hooks straight to his solar plexus. He even started to hunch over in pain, but pride made him straighten up real quick.

"Well, Lucy," he said evenly, "you've gotten everything you've wanted so far. Far be it from me to deprive you now."

"That's settled, then." Lucy's voice quivered.

"Settled." Mike's voice was unusually low.

Without another word, they both turned and headed inside the apartment, almost colliding at the patio door. Mike jumped back, fearing that just her touch might make him fall apart. Lucy hurried through the door, just as afraid of any physical contact with Mike, nervous that she might go to pieces on the spot.

The doors to the master bedroom and Mike's den slammed shut at the same time.

The Terrace of Apartment 1432C

EUNICE WAS sponging off the patio table as she and Clara heard a door slamming shut. "What do you want to bet that they're off together in the bedroom . . . You know what I'm saying," Eunice said, her hazel eyes sparkling.

Clara, who was plucking some dead leaves off a begonia plant, gave her companion a wry smile. "What do you want to bet they'll be back at each other's throats within two days' time?"

As it turned out, it was a good thing that Eunice didn't take Clara up on that bet. Eunice would have lost. Mike Powell moved out of apartment 1532C of the Harkness Towers on Central Park West that very morning.

"I WOULDN'T GO IN THERE if I were you."

Gwen, the wafer-thin model, who already had her hand on the doorknob leading into Lucy's office, looked over her shoulder at the svelte five-foot-ten woman who'd spoken, and frowned slightly. Not enough to produce any wrinkles, though. She was not about to blow her position as one of the leading cover girls at the Lucy Warner Modeling Agency by creating unphotogenic crease lines on her face. Or by walking in on the boss when she was in a bad mood. Lucy Warner's bad moods were legendary at the agency. The head honcho didn't have them often, but when she did, everyone within shooting distance knew to take cover.

Everyone, that is, except Lucy's best friend, Stephie Benson, who had offered Gwen the sage advice. Now a wife and mother, and weighing in at a good thirty pounds more than when she was in her prime as a model, Stephie wasn't one to always practice what she preached.

Gwen gingerly released her hand from the knob and stepped away from the door. Stephie gave her a motherly smile of approval and then walked past the model into Lucy's office without knocking.

"Go away," Lucy snarled, her back to the door.

"Are you this sweet and cheery every time you get divorced?" Stephie asked blithely, shutting the door behind her.

Lucy spun around in her swivel chair to face her old friend, the murderous expression on her face disintegrating on the spot. Dropping her head into the cradle of her arms on the desk, she moaned, "I feel sick."

"You look a little green around the gills," Stephie said, her wry New York voice holding a hint of sympathy. "Should I call your doctor or your lawyer?"

"If you're going to be . . . that way, you can go on home," Lucy murmured into the crook of her elbow.

"Okay," Stephie said airily.

Lucy's head popped up. "Don't you move from that spot."

Stephie didn't. She had no intention of deserting her friend in her hour of need. Even if she did think her friend needed to have her head examined. Stephie firmly believed that Mike Powell was the best thing that had ever happened to Lucy.

"You can call it off, you know," Stephie said, whisking a tissue out of her oversize tote bag and handing it to Lucy even before the tears started.

Lucy swept up the tissue. "I can't call it off. I...don't want to call it off."

"Even though you've been teetering between misery and despair since you and Mike split up?"

Lucy absently dabbed at the tears spiking her green eyes. "That isn't true. And even if it is, it doesn't mean this is a mistake. Mike certainly doesn't think it's a mistake."

"How do you know? Did he send you a fax to that effect?" Stephie took out another tissue, a rubber teething ring falling out of her tote in the process. She grabbed it up from the floor. "So that's where the darn thing went."

Lucy scowled as Stephie came around the desk, lifted her chin, and began rubbing off the black lines of mascara that were forming under Lucy's eyes.

"No, he hasn't sent me a fax," Lucy replied irritably, allowing the motherly ministrations. "He hasn't made the slightest attempt to communicate with me in any way. That's how I know."

"Oh, right. That makes a lot of sense, Lucy. You know Mike doesn't think this divorce nonsense is a big mistake because you haven't spoken one word to each other for the past two months."

"You're supposed to be on my side in this, Steph." There was such a pleading, desperate look on Lucy's face that Stephie immediately put her arms around her friend.

"I'm always on your side, kiddo," Stephie soothed.

"I'm getting mascara all over your beautiful blouse," Lucy mumbled.

"Don't worry. The mascara will just blend in with the oatmeal that Amy didn't like this morning. The joys of motherhood."

Lucy broke down in earnest. "I wouldn't know."

Stephie patted Lucy's back. "You're only twenty-eight, Luce. Your biological clock has plenty of ticking to go."

"No. It's not going to happen for me. I know it. I'm not going to be a mother. I'm never going to get married again, Steph. I'm not . . . good at it."

Stephie's lips curved in a smile. *Progress*, she thought. This was the first time in two months that Lucy had ever owned up to any of the responsibility for her failed marriage.

"It takes more than eight months of practice to get good at something as tough as marriage," Stephie said. "Believe me, I know. Jerry and I had plenty of rough spots along the way. Still do. But we did promise to stick it out for better or worse."

"You don't know how worse 'worse' can be," Lucy said softly, her finger absently running down the curve of her nose. And the worst part was that, once upon a time not so very long ago, she'd truly thought she and Mike were going to be the ideal married couple. They were so much in love. And then the differences between them hadn't been a barrier but an inducement. A perfect blending.

Lucy remembered their romantic wedding at that little church down in Greenwich Village. At first she'd wanted a big bash—one of those gala, star-studded society weddings with all the trimmings. However, Mike had convinced her that an intimate ceremony would be much more meaningful. She'd conceded to his wishes, and ended up being glad she had. Standing there at the altar beside Mike, she'd felt surrounded by love. Mike's Uncle Paulie was best man, a few close friends sat in attendance, and her mother and stepfather, a British diplomat, flew in from London where Lucy had spent much of her adolescence. Lucy fought back tears, as she recalled her mother's words to her right after the ceremony. "He's so right for you, Lucy. I never thought you'd have the good sense to marry a man like Mike." A lot her mother knew. Good sense, indeed!

After observing Lucy for a minute, Stephie checked her watch. "You could give him a call, Luce. He's probably still at his office. Just talk to him before you go over to the courthouse, get a feel for where he's at."

Lucy sniffed back tears, blew her nose into a tissue then pulled herself together. "No. I am not calling Mike. I don't know what's come over me. I was fine when I got up this morning. I've been fine for two months." Lucy held up her hand. "Okay, okay. Maybe *fine* is too strong a word. I've been coping."

"Coping," Stephie echoed wryly. "That's one of those words that you always see in self-help books. Personally, I don't think anyone knows what the word means."

Lucy produced a smile as phony as a three-dollar bill. "I knew it was a smart move, asking you to come along to the courthouse with me. See, you're cheering me up already."

Stephie shook her head. "Why run a two-bit modeling agency when you could go on Broadway as the next Sarah Bernhardt?"

Lucy's temper flared. "This is not a two-bit agency, and if you . . ."

Stephie grinned. "That's better. Keep your emotions honest, kiddo, and, like Confucius says, your dreams will come true."

"Fortune-cookie philosophy," Lucy said dryly. "Just what I need."

Stephie pulled Lucy to her feet. "No, what you need is to go powder your nose and do something about those bloodshot eyes. If we're heading for the courthouse, I'm sure you'll want to look your best. For the judge."

"Very funny."

"On the other hand, we can skip the courthouse and just go pig out at some chic, pricey uptown restaurant?"

Lucy was already heading to her private bathroom. She tossed back her hair, glanced over her shoulder, and gave her friend an unflappable look. "Funny, funny, funny. I'm going to laugh all the way over to the courthouse."

"I'LL HAVE A SCOTCH. Neat."

The big, ruddy, gray-haired man behind the bar looked incredulous. "Mikey, Mikey. What are you talking about? It's eleven o'clock in the morning."

"So, you don't sell booze at eleven in the morning? Give me the Scotch, Uncle Paulie. And, please, can the man-to-man speech you're about to give me."

"Man-to-man? You're growing younger by the minute, Mikey. Right now, I'd say you're hovering between adolescence and prepuberty."

"That's what happens to a guy after eight months of marriage to Lucy Warner. Her immaturity must have been contagious."

Uncle Paulie rubbed his hands along the icy-smooth, cool black marble-topped bar. "Well, maybe you're right. Lucy was pretty childish."

"Childish? Did I tell you about the plate of scrambled eggs she shoved in my face?" Mike said irritably.

"Only a couple of hundred times. But, if it makes you feel better, kid, go on and tell me again."

Mike scowled. "Forget it." He shook his head. "Boy, that plateful of eggs was the finishing touch. The straw that broke this camel's back. I mean it, Uncle Paulie. Does a reasonable wife decorate her husband's face with a plateful of scrambled eggs? Does she?"

Uncle Paulie shrugged. "What do I know about wives, Mikey? I'm a bachelor, remember?"

"Well, I'll tell you. A reasonable wife does not stuff a plateful of scrambled eggs in her husband's face. You take it from me."

"Okay, look at the bright side. They could have been fried eggs with undercooked yokes."

Mike scowled at his uncle. "Very amusing."

"So, what time did you say you were due at the courthouse?"

"Eleven-thirty. Knowing Lucy, she'll be a half-hour late, anyway. Lucy's never on time."

"Childish, never on time, throws her breakfast in your face. Tell me, Mikey, what'd you ever see in that nutty dame?"

"You make it sound like she had no redeeming qualities," he said churlishly.

Uncle Paulie leaned over and rested his elbows on the bar. "She had redeeming qualities? Name three."

"Sure, I'll name three," Mike rejoindered. "One, she's ravishingly beautiful, smart as a whip, funny, inventive, provocative, clever, affectionate, sexy." He took a breath. "And three, there was never a dull moment around Lucy."

Uncle Paulie faked a cough into his sleeve so that his nephew wouldn't see him smiling. "Like you said, though, the two of you just didn't mix. Oil and water, right, Mike? I guess there was some fun in the shaking. While it lasted."

"It was great while it lasted. We were running in circles, though. I was always . . . dizzy. You can't function, Uncle Paulie, if you're always dizzy."

The older man patted his nephew's arm. It broke his heart that Mike and Lucy had split up. Like everyone else who knew them well, he thought they were ideally suited. And Paulie knew there'd been a time when Lucy and Mike had thought so, too. In Paulie's opinion, Lucy was just what his nephew needed. She loosened him up a little. And Mike needed some loosening up. He was too conservative, too cautious, too worried about money and image. Not that Mike didn't have some justification, Paulie conceded. First the kid's mom passed away when the kid was only seven and then two years later his dad took off for parts unknown, never to be seen or heard from again. Then Mikey ended up being raised by a no-account bachelor uncle who owned a broken-down jazz club in a seedy Greenwich Village neighborhood.

Paulie smiled, looking around at the now classy Bennett Street Club & Grill, which featured the best jazz musicians around town and some good down-home cooking. He owed his success to Mike and his business acumen. Eight years ago, Paulie had almost sold the place for what looked to him at the time to be a sweet profit. What he hadn't realized was that the neighborhood was going through a transition. A couple of slick investors thought they could get in cheap, fix the place up and as the neighborhood got more and more upscale, re-sell and make a real killing. It was Mike, then newly out of business school, who had talked his uncle into holding on to the property. Within a year, he'd helped Paulie turn the club into a money-making proposition. Now, Paulie was sitting on easy street for the first time in his life. He owed it all to Mike. And it was a debt he didn't take likely. There was nothing he wouldn't do for his nephew to repay him.

"Well, I guess this is where I get off the merry-go-round ride for good," Mike muttered wistfully, drawing his uncle out of his reverie.

"You could always buy another strip of tickets," Paulie interjected only half-jokingly. One of Mike's other qualities that served as both an asset and a hazard was that he was so single-minded. Once he got something in his head, it stuck there like Krazy Glue.

"We both agreed it was our only option," Mike said fatalistically. "We were driving each other crazy. Total opposites. We were all wrong for each other."

"If you say so, Mikey," Paulie said without much conviction.

Mike's gaze drifted off. "Not that there are any hard feelings. I mean, Lucy's an . . . incredible woman. Vivacious, irrepressible, luminous. Sultry as all get-out."

"Here," Uncle Paulie said sympathetically.

Mike stared at the glass of Scotch his uncle had set before him. "No. It's crazy. I don't drink hard liquor at eleven o'clock in the morning. Hell, I don't drink it any time of day. I hate the stuff."

Uncle Paulie gave his nephew a sage smile. "Yeah. I know. This is one morning to make an exception. Drink up."

Mike hesitated, then downed the Scotch in one long gulp. It burned going down. But it helped. A little.

THEY CAME OUT OF THE courthouse together, each of them holding a yellow manila envelope containing the official divorce decree between Michael Lloyd Powell and Lucy Warner Powell. They started down the steps, Stephie hanging back a fair distance.

"Well," Lucy muttered, her violet-painted nails tapping the envelope.

"Well," Mike echoed, moving to stick his envelope in his inside jacket pocket only to discover that it didn't fit. He thought to himself that if he had more of a psychological bent, he might have made something of that.

They started down the wide concrete steps outside the courthouse. Stephie hung back a little more.

Lucy shot Mike a look, just as he was turning to check her out. Caught in the act, they both smiled awkwardly.

He looks thinner, Lucy thought.

"You look good, Mike."

She looks paler, Mike thought.

"You, too, Lucy. You look great."

Their steps slowed even more.

"So, how've you been doing?" Lucy asked in a measured voice.

"Great. Super. Just . . . great," Mike said, cursing himself for sounding overeager to be convincing. "And you?"

"Oh, the same. Busy. Very busy. The business, and all," Lucy muttered. *Spoken just like a brilliant businesswoman. Not!*

"Good. Nothing wrong with being busy. I'm real busy, too. It's crazy. Sometimes, I even find myself dreaming about figures at night. I mean . . . *number* figures."

Stephie, five steps back, rolled her eyes.

Lucy and Mike both hesitated on the last step. As if they each knew that once their feet touched down on the sidewalk, they'd be going their separate ways. For good.

Lucy could feel her heart racing as she glanced quickly at Mike.

He looks sad, she thought. *And lonely.*

Just as she turned her head away, Mike shot her a glance.

She looks like she hasn't been getting much sleep, he thought.

"Well . . . listen," Lucy muttered, "take care of yourself."

"Right," Mike mumbled. "You, too."

They still didn't budge from the step. Stephie remained poised a few steps behind, observing the pair and shaking her head.

Does he have any feelings left for me at all? Lucy wondered.

Does she feel anything but relief that it's over and done with? Mike wondered.

"Oh, Mike. About those CDs you left at the apartment. If you want them back—"

"That's okay. You can keep them. You always liked them better than I did."

Lucy somehow managed the closest she could come to a gracious smile. "Thanks." *This proves he never wants to see me again. I gave him an opening and he slammed the door right in my face.*

Mike gave a breezy little smile that took all his effort. *She can't even stand to have any of my things around the place. Wants to just wipe out all evidence I ever existed in her life.*

"So . . . take care, Mike." Lucy frowned. *Didn't I say that already?*

"Right. You, too, Lucy."

She turned slightly to face him. "No hard feelings." She threw out her hand.

He turned toward her, saw her extended hand, hesitated, then shook it formally. "No. Right. No hard feelings. None. Absolutely none." *Okay, already. You made your point. Now shut up. And let go of her hand, you idiot.*

"I mean, we both agree it was the smartest decision we could have made. Under the circumstances."

"Yes," Mike said, deciding to stick to monosyllables as a way to stop running off at the mouth and sounding like a complete jerk.

Lucy's nails did another rat-a-tat-tat on the manila envelope. "So . . . keep in touch, Mike."

"Yeah. You, too."

I won't call him first if my life depends on it, Lucy vowed.

If she thinks I'm going to make the first move, she's whistling Dixie, Mike swore.

Stephie was fast running out of patience with these two. Just as they were finally running out of banal chitchat and saw that they had no option but to move off that step down onto the sidewalk, she picked up her pace and wedged herself in between them.

"Oh," Stephie moaned convincingly, grabbing onto each of their arms. "Oh, I feel a little . . . odd."

"Odd?" Lucy anxiously asked her friend. "You feel odd?" She looked at Mike. "She feels odd."

"How do you mean . . . odd?" Mike asked Stephie.

Stephie tightened her grip on their sleeves. "Maybe it was that tutti-frutti ice cream I ate last night. Or the sausage patty I had for breakfast. Or it could just be some kind of a flu. Or...something." Stephie swayed slightly and leaned against Mike.

"Get a cab for us, Lucy," Mike said, putting a supporting arm around Stephie's waist. "We'll take you to the hospital, Steph."

"No. I don't need to go to a hospital. But if you could just both help me home, I'd . . . really appreciate it."

Lucy spotted a taxi and raced to the curb, flagging it down. Stephie let Mike lead her manfully into the cab. He scooted in on one side of her. Lucy was on her other side.

"You're sure you don't want to go to the hospital?" Lucy asked, taking hold of Stephie's hand.

Stephie felt a flash of guilt, but she quickly told herself that in this case the end justified the means. "No, really. I'm a little better. Maybe I just need to eat something. And the baby-sitter's expecting me back."

"I'll stay with you," Lucy said. "You're in no condition to look after a two-year-old on your own."

"You're being silly," Stephie replied, smiling weakly. "I tell you what. The two of you can stick around for lunch, and then if I don't feel any better, I'll give Jerry a ring and he can come home early and look after me."

Lucy and Mike glanced at each other. They were both thinking the same thing. Once upon a time they would have had each other to look after them if they were sick. That time, however, had come and gone.

They focused back on Stephie. Stephie smiled. "Gee, guys, thanks a lot for . . . this. I know it must be kind of awkward for you."

"No," they lied in unison.

Stephie gave each of them a little pat. "I just want you to know I appreciate it."

STEPHIE WALKED INTO HER kitchen and picked up a note lying on the table. "Will you look at this? A note from my sitter. She thought I might be late and decided to take Amy over to the park for lunch."

Lucy and Mike stood almost shoulder to shoulder at the kitchen door.

"Well, that's nice," Lucy said. "I mean . . . it's a break for you."

Mike nodded. "Give you a chance to . . . catch your breath." His own breath needed some catching, as well.

Stephie eyed them both. "Look, I think I'll just go lie down for a little while. There's some fabulous leftover roast beef in the fridge and plenty of Jerry's famous potato salad. Help yourselves. Somebody might as well enjoy it all."

Before either of them could argue, Stephie had pulled them both into the kitchen and made a hasty exit.

"Jerry does make terrific potato salad," Lucy said.

Mike nodded. "Didn't he bring some over to our house for our—" He stopped abruptly.

"Our anniversary party," Lucy said, filling in the rest. "Yes." She gave a mirthless little laugh. "I guess it was just as well we celebrated at six months, seeing as how we didn't make it to a year."

Mike groped for an image to replace the one that was forming in his mind—the image of Lucy entwined in his arms after that anniversary party.

"Now we can really celebrate," she'd said seductively that night as they embraced in the middle of the living room. Then her hand had cruised lightly, provocatively down the front of his trousers as she swayed in his arms to a bluesy Sinatra tune on the CD player.

"Dance with me," she'd murmured.

"I'm a lousy dancer," he'd said.

"Tonight, baby, you're going to be Fred Astaire."

Funny thing was, he'd almost felt like Fred Astaire that night. Not that he'd ever seen Astaire dancing naked in any of his movies—with a naked Ginger Rogers on his arm, no less. That night, Lucy's clever, enticing moves had put old Ginger to shame. What a dance that was....

"Did you just say something about a dance?" Lucy asked. She was at the fridge pulling out plastic containers of leftovers.

Mike felt his cheeks heat up. "No. No. I ... uh ... said, is there any mustard by any ... chance?"

"Since when do you like mustard on roast beef? You always use mayonnaise," Lucy countered.

A good point. He hated mustard on roast beef. He hated mustard on anything but a hot dog. "Not anymore. Cholesterol, you know. And the calories. Got to stay in shape. Amazing how quickly the body starts to deteriorate if you don't . . . uh . . . take care of it."

Lucy felt her temperature start to rise. Was that a not-so-subtle hint that she wasn't in shape? Okay, so she'd lost a few pounds over the past couple of months. Going through a divorce wasn't exactly a picnic. Still, at one hundred and twenty-five pounds she wasn't exactly emaciated. Compared to her models, she was practically . . . plump.

She made up a huge sandwich, ladled two heaping spoonfuls of potato salad on her plate and shoved the container across the kitchen table to Mike.

"Help yourself," she said snippily.

Mike was bewildered by her mood swing. Had he said something wrong? Was she suspicious about his sudden preference for mustard? Did she guess he'd been remembering their erotic sixth-month-anniversary dance? Did *she* remember?

"I'm really not that hungry," he muttered, staring into the container of potato salad.

"Really?" Lucy said, putting her two hands around her mile-high roast-beef sandwich. "I'm just starved." A total lie. She'd completely lost her appetite. The thought of biting into that sandwich totally nauseated her. She was tempted to barge into Stephie's bedroom and tell her to move over. *She* felt odd, too.

She set the sandwich down on her plate and stared at Mike across the table. "This *is* . . . awkward. Sitting here together, having lunch. As if nothing has happened."

"I don't think either of us is acting like nothing's happened, Lucy," Mike said quietly.

"No," Lucy agreed in a bare whisper. She felt a jagged edge of pain in the pit of her stomach.

He reached across the table and squeezed her hand. "I want you to know, Lucy, that I hope one of these days you find the right guy for you."

She squeezed back. "You, too, Mike. I mean, I hope you find the right kind of woman. Someone . . . traditional, conventional, even-tempered, prompt. . . ."

Mike abruptly released her hand. "I'm not exactly in the market for a drone," he said tightly.

Lucy cleared her throat. "Oh? What kind of woman are you in the market for this time around?"

Mike edged his plate away and folded his hands on the table. His knuckles turned white. "I thought I'd let the divorce papers age for a few days before I got into the market again."

Lucy shoved aside her plate. "Well, when you said you weren't exactly in the market for a drone, the inference was you *were* in the market. I just presumed, anyway."

"I'll tell you one thing I will be in the market for, when I choose to enter the market. And that's a woman who doesn't presume."

She leaned forward, pressing both palms flat on the table. "Right. Next time, go for a *dumb* blonde. One who's too stupid to have a thought of her own, an ounce of creativity or spontaneity. A placid, meek, miserly little blonde . . ."

Mike could feel his blood pressure start to rise. "And what kind of a guy are you going to be in the market for this time around, Lucy? Some crass, flashy, narcissistic artist or actor type who wears black leather pants and rides a motorcycle? Of course, he'd have to be a rich artist—the way you like to throw money around. Not to mention china."

"If what you're trying to say is that next time I'll pick someone who's got some real spirit, never wears a blue suit if he can help it, and likes to live a little dangerously, you couldn't be more right."

"Well, believe me," Mike retorted, feeling himself start to flush, "the next woman I get involved with is going to be mature, responsible, sensitive to other people's feelings—"

"Are you implying that I'm not sensitive?"

"See how well you listen? I wasn't implying. I was stating a fact."

Lucy's mouth twitched. "I see. A fact." With amazing self-containment she rose from her chair.

Mike did likewise. Things were getting completely out of hand. As usual. He decided to try to reason with her. Why, he didn't know, since he'd never had any luck reasoning with her in the past.

"Now, look, Lucy. This is pretty crazy. We got divorced so we wouldn't get into these ridiculous squabbles."

"Ridiculous? You call me insensitive, irresponsible, immature, and then you say I'm being ridiculous?"

"I didn't say *you* were being ridiculous. I called the squabble ridiculous."

Lucy's fine nostrils flared. "Well, I guess I just wasn't listening again."

"See, Lucy, you always take things one step over the line."

"Do I?" Lucy snapped, grabbing up the container of potato salad. "One step over the line? Only *one* step?"

Mike gave first the container and then his ex-wife of less than an hour a wary look. "Lucy, I'm warning you—"

Stephie was just outside the kitchen, saying, "I feel a little better. Maybe I'll have a bite to eat after—" She stopped dead in her tracks at the kitchen door and stared openmouthed at

Mike, whose hair was coated with potato salad. "What the—?"

"I hope you don't want potato salad," Lucy said airily, gathering up her purse and marching right past Stephie. "There isn't any left."

2

"LUCY," PENELOPE LAINE drawled, bussing her on both cheeks. "You look fantastic. I'm so glad you could come to the bash. It's been ages."

Lucy smiled. "Yes, it has." She half turned to the exotic-looking, long-haired man standing beside her. "Pen, this is—"

"Martin McGann needs no introduction, Lucy," Penelope gushed, taking hold of the famous Broadway director's hand. "This is a real honor, Mr. McGann. Why, only last Saturday night my husband, Tom, and I saw your new play, *Warm Heart, Cold Feet,* at the Majestic. What can I say? I laughed. I cried. It's your best. Positively your best." The hostess glanced at Lucy. "Don't you agree?"

"Well, actually," Lucy said, "I haven't had a chance—"

"Oh, you must," Penelope exclaimed, cutting Lucy off. "Everyone in town has seen it by now."

Lucy stiffened as her date put his arm around her waist and gave her a provocative smile.

"I've been saying the same thing, Lucy," Martin McGann drawled with a hint of an Irish brogue. "You've got to come see it. Oh, I don't know if I'd say *Warm Heart, Cold Feet,* is my best work, but it's right up there with *Crossing Over* and *Granting Wishes.*"

"Is it?" Lucy said, trying to act like what he was saying was of any interest at all to her.

"Lucy," he scolded lightly, "don't tell me you haven't seen either *Crossing Over* or *Granting Wishes?*"

There was one wish Lucy would have loved someone to grant her at that moment—the wish that the egotistical Martin McGann would disappear. What had she been thinking when she invited him out tonight? The man was a bona fide narcissist. It was only that he'd been pestering her for weeks, and she hadn't wanted to come to the party alone. Actually, she hadn't wanted to come at all. She'd only showed up to convince Stephie that she wasn't still "moping around" because of the divorce. She discreetly scanned the elegant living room—where well-dressed, well-heeled people who all projected that savvy air of success were clustered in little groups chatting—looking for Stephie and Jerry.

"The only excuse you can give me for not seeing even one of my three best works is that you've been abroad for the past three years," Martin went on in a mockingly gruff voice that Lucy found intensely irritating.

"I was abroad for the past three years," Lucy said, deadpan.

The hostess, who'd turned briefly to greet some other guests, turned back to Lucy and Martin.

"My husband's going to be absolutely thrilled to meet you, Mr. McGann." She smiled coyly. "Or may I call you Martin?"

The director, not so much handsome as striking looking, gave the hostess a playful smile, then stroked the red silk scarf he wore over his fringed suede cowboy jacket. "Anyone who showers my work with such praise must call me Marty."

The hostess was thrilled. "Then you must call me Penny." Again she smiled coyly. "Get it? Penny Laine. You know. Like the Beatles song. Only not spelled the same way—the Laine part." She lunged for the director's sleeve. "Oh, there's Tom. Lucy, may I borrow Marty for a minute? Tom is just going to die...."

"Oh . . . sure. Sure. Be my guest," Lucy muttered, already bored and sorry she'd come to the party. She should have opted for moping.

Stephie came up behind her. "Why did you ever talk me into this? This is the worst party I've been to since . . . since her last one."

"*You* talked *me* into this, remember?" Lucy murmured acerbically. "And now that I think about it, didn't we swear after Penny's last dreary bash that we'd both find some excuse when we got our next invitations?"

"You're right," Stephie said. "Jerry and I were going to say we'd won a trip to Acapulco, and you and Mike were going to say that you'd signed up for mambo lessons." Stephie grinned. "I can't picture Mike doing the mambo."

Lucy stared down at the Oriental rug. "I don't know," she said in a low voice. "He wasn't really all that bad a dancer. There were times . . ." One time in particular.

"Where is lover boy?" Stephie quipped.

Lucy looked across the room and gasped. "Oh, God, he's over there."

Stephie was baffled until she followed Lucy's gaze. "What do you know. It's Mike." She withdrew a pair of silver-rimmed glasses from her purse. "Who's that with him?"

Lucy shoved Stephie in front of her. "I don't know who she is. I don't want to know. I knew I shouldn't have come tonight. This is all your fault, Steph."

"She looks very Brooks Brothers," Stephie went on blithely, continuing her study of Mike's date.

"Will you stop staring? I've got to find Martin and tell him I've got a headache."

"Oh, don't be such a wimp, Luce," Stephie chided. "It's been . . . what, a month or more since he took that potato-salad shower?"

Lucy groaned. "I swear that man brought out the beast in me."

Stephie grinned. "I bet he did."

"Shut up," Lucy snapped. "Is she pretty?"

Stephie's grin broadened. "She's okay in a crisp, polished sort of way. I'd wager a fellow accountant or maybe a lawyer."

"Will you stop staring," Lucy said edgily.

"You asked me if she was pretty. How am I supposed to answer if I don't look at her?"

"Okay, okay. You looked. Now, listen, Steph. You go find Martin for me and tell him I'm out in the hall waiting for him because of this terrible headache that I really am getting—"

"I don't know what Martin looks like—"

"He's got black hair down to his shoulders and he looks just like you'd imagine a Broadway director would look like. You can't miss him. Anyway, Penny's got him in her clutches. All you have to do is find her."

Too late. "Mike and his lady friend are heading in this—" Stephie said, talking faster.

"Hi, Stephie."

Stephie did a sidestep as she smiled a greeting to Mike.

Lucy came into full view.

Mike blanched. "Lucy."

Lucy's coloring also took a nosedive. "Mike."

Stephie gave a little wave and floated off.

Neither Lucy nor Mike noticed her gesture or her departure. They just stood there motionless, their hearts racing, staring at each other in awkward silence until the trim, very attractive brunette in a tailored silk taupe dress slipped her arm through Mike's, making him suddenly remember her.

"Oh, Lucy, this is..." For a brief second he forgot his date's name. Something like Ruth. Rose? "Royce." He gave his date a quick look to make sure he'd got it right. She seemed satisfied. But then she wasn't exactly the most expressive woman he'd ever come across, so it was hard to really tell.

Royce extended her hand to Lucy. "Nice to meet you. Are you and Mike old friends?"

"Oh, no," Lucy said without thinking.

Mike smoothed down his already wrinkle-free blue jacket. "We . . . we're . . . That is, Lucy and I used to be . . ."

"Married," Lucy finished for him, grabbing a goblet of champagne off a tray being carried around by a waiter. "Very briefly. It was . . . just one of those things. We kind of rushed into it and . . . rushed out."

"It happens," Mike mumbled, distracted by the scent of Lucy's perfume. It had been a long time since he'd smelled that heady tropical scent. It made him suddenly dizzy with memory.

Royce smiled placidly. "It's a pity."

They both stared at her.

"It's a pity that people in general take marriage so casually," Royce said loftily. "Why, if we ever behaved as impulsively and cavalierly in business as we do in our personal relationships we'd all be on the unemployment lines." She gave a little laugh.

Mike cleared his throat and Lucy contemplated dumping her glass of champagne over the woman's head but she controlled herself. Barely.

To add to Lucy's irritation, discomfort and misery, Marty showed up, throwing his arm around her and giving her a squeeze. "You naughty girl. Leaving me to fend for myself like that. You know how I hate people fawning over me. It absolutely embarrasses me."

Lucy didn't know anything of the sort. She hardly knew Martin McGann and would have preferred knowing him even less. But she wasn't about to let on about that in front of Mike and his *perfect match.*

"Oh, darling. I'm sorry," Lucy gushed in a pretty good imitation of Penny. "I would have rescued you, but I was here talking with—" she swept a glance past Mike and Royce "—my ex-husband and his . . . friend, Rose."

"Royce," Mike's date corrected tartly.

"Funny," Marty mused. "I wouldn't have ever pictured the two of you as husband and wife."

"We didn't picture it too well, either, obviously," Lucy quipped.

"No," Mike said tightly. "we weren't your usual picture-perfect pair." He jumped back abruptly as he saw Lucy raise her champagne glass. She merely brought it to her lips—lips that bore a faintly amused smile.

Marty's hand sauntered from Lucy's shoulder to her neck, which he began to massage seductively. "Some lady told me you wanted to leave because you'd come down with a sudden headache."

"Headache?" Lucy repeated with feigned surprise. "Me? No. She must have gotten me confused with someone else. I feel terrific. Great." She smiled brightly at Mike, slipping her arm around Marty's waist. "Wonderful." She kept the smile glued on her face as she saw Mike take affectionate hold of Royce's hand. What kind of name was Royce? Lucy thought irritably. It was so . . . pretentious.

Later, Lucy corralled Stephie in one of the guest bathrooms. "Well, all I can say is they deserve each other," Lucy said airily. "I knew he'd wind up with some cool, snooty junior exec. She's perfect. Absolutely perfect for him. He certainly seems content. And she obviously thinks he's a good catch. And he is. For her. For someone like her. Although, if you ask me, he could do better. I didn't get the feeling she was all that bright. I got the distinct impression that there wasn't much light at the end of that tunnel. And that dress. I mean, it's fine for a business luncheon or something like that, but for a party? It's so . . . dour." Lucy glanced at her reflection in the mirror, taking in her swingy rayon-jersey dress in multi-rows of vibrant colors. "I suppose *Royce* thinks I'm over-dressed. And tastelessly flashy. Probably Mike does, too." She frowned.

Stephie grinned at Lucy's mirror image. "You sure that's all you have to say?"

"What's that supposed to mean?" Lucy's frown deepened. "Okay, so I got a little thrown, seeing him again."

"You mean seeing him with a date."

"You're so smart, Ms. Freud. Okay, it did shake me up a bit to see him with . . . with someone else. It's only been a little over a month since the divorce. He told me he wasn't going to rush into the dating scene again."

"You're here with someone else, too," Stephie pointed out.

"It's not the same thing. I can't stand Martin McGann. He's vain, pretentious, obnoxious, and he keeps trying to paw me like I'm a cross between his pet dog and a Barbie doll."

Stephie grinned. "Gee, the two of you seemed pretty chummy out there."

"If you think I was trying to make Mike jealous, you're wrong," Lucy snapped.

"I don't think that. I think you were determined to show Mike that your heart wasn't breaking. If it makes you feel any better, you probably succeeded."

Lucy sighed. What was the point of trying to put something over on Stephie? Her friend always had read her like a book. "It doesn't make me feel any better."

Stephie put a comforting arm around her friend's shoulders. "I had a little chat with the junior exec. This is her first date with Mike. If he's got any smarts at all, it'll be his last. She's a real dud."

Lucy put her head on Stephie's shoulder. "You're a good friend."

"Does that mean you finally forgive me for orchestrating the infamous post-divorce potato-salad fiasco?"

Lucy sighed. "I forgive you. I doubt whether Mike will ever forgive me."

"*WARM HEART, COLD FEET?*" Paulie shook his head. "Never heard of it. Sounds like a run-in to a TV commercial."

"It's a hit Broadway play," Mike said mordantly, sipping a club soda at the bar while his uncle finished closing up for the night. "Lucy's dating the director."

Paulie looked up from the cash register. "You saw her?"

Mike nodded. "Earlier this evening. At a party. She was with him." He sighed. "I knew she'd wind up with someone like that. I predicted it. I could have bet millions on it—if I were the betting kind."

"So, what was he like?" Paulie asked, shutting the register drawer.

Mike made a face. "Oh, you know the sort. Flashy in that baroque sort of way, oozing with dramatic charm, hair down to his navel, flowing scarves, leather pants, cowboy jacket. They probably arrived on his motorcycle. Or on his horse. Lucy was falling all over him. She was practically panting. If you ask me, it was a little...inappropriate."

Mike took a swallow of club soda. "Well, all I can say is, I wish her luck. Personally, though, I think she could do better. A lot better. He probably has a string of women. Half the women at the party were coming on to him."

"Your date included?" Paulie asked casually.

"Royce Woodrow? Hardly," Mike said with a sardonic grin. "She's so straight-arrow I felt like I was getting jabbed every time she got too close."

Paulie bit back a smile.

"I don't know why I ever asked her out. Oh, I guess I was impressed by the presentation she gave at that conference I went to last month. And I didn't want to ask anyone out from work. It can get sticky. And—"

"And you didn't want to show up without a date to a party that Lucy was likely to be attending?" Paulie suggested.

"It had nothing to do with Lucy," Mike said defensively. "I just thought I ought to start . . . going out, meeting people . . . women." He stared into his club soda. "Maybe it did cross my mind that she might be there." His eyes shot up to his uncle, who quickly donned a straight face. "I didn't think it was likely. Just a possibility."

His uncle held his gaze. "Mikey, Mikey, Mikey."

"She did look terrific," Mike said wistfully. "Always could stand out in a crowd." He ran his finger lightly around the rim of his glass. "Oh, the dress she had on was wild, typically Lucy, but she's got what it takes to pull it off." He pictured her at the party, standing beside that long-haired, self-centered, effete jerk, their arms entwined around each other, her smile curling around him in a conspiratorial embrace. The image made Mike wince.

"You okay?" Paulie asked, leaning over the bar to rest a hand on his nephew's shoulder.

Mike smiled. "Sure. I'm fine."

"If you say so." Paulie shrugged, clearly not convinced.

Mike's smile drooped. "It's the irony of it, Uncle Paulie. I couldn't live with her, that was for sure. But, now I can't seem to live too well without her, either."

"Well, kid, looks like that leaves you one of two choices. I know which one I'd make."

Mike wore a mournful expression. "You're wrong, Uncle Paulie. There are no choices. I saw that tonight."

"Maybe," Paulie suggested, "you only saw what Lucy wanted you to see. Just like maybe *she* saw only what you *wanted* her to see."

"You mean Rose?"

"I thought you said her name was Royce."

Mike grinned. "Was it?"

THE NEXT TIME LUCY and Mike tangled, quite literally, was at the busy dry cleaners at Broadway and Eighty-sixth Street just a few blocks west of the Harkness Towers. Lucy was in one line getting her cleaning and Mike was two lines down, picking up his. They connected, or rather their hangers connected, by the door.

"Mike."

"Lucy."

They stared at the intertwined hangers, each nervously reaching at the same time to try to disentangle them. Their hands touched. Their heads jerked up and they both flushed.

"Here, let me," Mike said huskily.

Lucy nodded mutely.

He was all thumbs, but he finally managed the task. They remained standing at the door, not saying anything.

"Excuse me," a woman, loaded down with a drop-off, said irritably as she bustled into the shop and nearly collided with them.

They stepped outside and moved away from the entrance.

"What are you doing in the neighborhood?" Lucy asked, forcing the kind of offhanded tone she'd use with the post-man.

"I live here," Mike said. He realized he was staring and pulled his gaze away, giving the street a random survey.

"Oh. I thought you'd moved down to the Village."

"That was just temporary. I've got an apartment a couple of blocks down. On Eighty-fourth."

"Oh. Well, that's a...good street. Convenient. I mean...for the subway."

"Right. I thought so. The building's not bad. Pre-World War II. Very solid. Well built." His eyes drifted of their own accord down his ex-wife's body. She was wearing a pair of tight jeans and a brown leather bomber jacket that hugged her narrow hips, its masculine cut accentuating her sensuality. Her blond hair was tied back from her face, a few loose tendrils floating with the autumn breeze. She wasn't wearing any makeup. She didn't need any. Her fresh-scrubbed complexion glowed.

Laughter from a couple of passersby brought Mike up short. He pretended interest in them as they walked by.

"How are you and . . . what's his name doing?" he muttered, turning his attention back to Lucy.

For a moment, Lucy drew a blank. "Oh. You mean Marty. Oh, well . . . I guess he's doing fine."

"You're not . . . still seeing him then?"

"Oh. Oh, I see him . . . sometimes," she lied unabashedly. "Not too often. What with his directing and all. You've seen . . . *Warm Feet, Cold Heart*, haven't you? Everyone in town has."

"You mean *Warm Heart, Cold Feet*, don't you?" Mike replied.

Lucy flushed. "Oh, isn't that what I said?" She gave an artificial laugh. "Well, maybe I was thinking of his sequel."

Mike grinned.

Lucy swept a strand of hair off her cheek. "What about you and . . . ?"

"Rose? Oh, she's great. Not that we get together all that much. We see each other and all, but we've both got . . . busy schedules."

Lucy eyed him. "I thought her name was Royce."

Mike flushed. "Well, actually, I haven't seen her . . . for a while."

Lucy smiled, her arms getting a bit tired from the weight of the dry cleaning that was draped over them. "Yeah. Well, I haven't seen Marty recently. And to tell you the truth I haven't gotten around to seeing his play yet, whatever it's called."

Mike grinned. "The reviews weren't all that great." He'd actually gone to the library the day after that party and looked them up.

Lucy grinned back, readjusting her armload of pressed clothes.

"Why don't you throw them over mine?" Mike suggested impulsively. "I'm walking your way. And it's been a long time since I've carried home a gal's dry cleaning for her."

Lucy knew the wisest thing for her to do would have been to politely say, "No, thanks." Why go looking for trouble just when she'd finally begun to accept the reality of their divorce?

Mike got edgy when she hesitated, chiding himself for overstepping the line. He'd sworn to himself when he moved back to the old neighborhood, that if he did happen to run into Lucy he would be cordial but distant. So, what was he doing, offering to carry her clothes home from the dry cleaner's for her? He felt like a goofy teenager asking the most popular girl in school if he could carry her books home.

Just as Lucy was about to accept his offer—she never had been famous for making wise moves—Mike took her delay for a no.

"Actually, I do have another stop to make, anyway," he mumbled, trying not to sound hurt by her lack of response.

He didn't have to worry. Lucy was too busy feeling rejected. "Oh, that's okay. That's fine. The stuff is light. Actually I'm in a hurry. I've got to meet someone for lunch. Downtown." A phony smile blinked on and off. "You know how men hate to be kept waiting."

Mike gave her a strained look. "Yeah, I know."

Again, she shifted the dry cleaning in her arms. Now it was her lies, not the clothes, that were starting to weigh heavily on her. Why had she made up that dumb story about a luncheon date?

LUCY EXAMINED A PERFECTLY clean sweater, deciding that it really did need to be dry-cleaned. She'd drop it off on her way home from work. Yesterday, it had been a wool skirt. A couple of days before that, she'd decided to bring in her down parka. Okay, so she wasn't likely to be going skiing in mid-September. Maybe she was turning over a new leaf, getting more organized, planning ahead. Or maybe she was just hoping to tangle hangers again with an ex-husband by the name of Mike Powell.

She knew things were getting out of hand. For the past five days, ever since she'd bumped into Mike in the dry cleaner's and learned he was in the neighborhood, she'd suddenly taken to frequenting not just the dry cleaner's on an almost-daily basis, but the local grocery store, the hardware store, the bank, and just about every shop in the neighborhood that she imagined Mike might frequent.

Okay, so she wanted to run into him again. A kind of desensitization technique she'd read about somewhere. Probably in *Cosmo*. Probably an article about "coping" with divorce.

Lucy tried to tell herself that she just needed to get used to seeing Mike around so when they did bump into each other it wouldn't be so awkward and uncomfortable. Like it had been that evening at Penny's. And then again at the dry cleaner's. Their two inadvertent encounters since the divorce had thrown her off for days. She'd had trouble concentrating. She'd had trouble sleeping. Mike kept popping up in her dreams. She had to exorcise him.

Gathering up her sweater for the dry cleaner's in one hand and her attaché case in her other, she was about to leave her office when her bookkeeper, Emily Thomas, walked in, carrying a large ledger.

"These are the six-month figures," Emily said, then hesitated. "They're ready for . . . the accountant."

Lucy set her attaché case back down on her desk. "Oh." She scowled.

"Are we going to . . . still use your . . . I mean, Mr. Powell?" Emily asked quietly.

Lucy sighed and massaged her neck, the muscles suddenly going tight. Her gaze drifted to the day calendar on her desk, only now really taking in the date. September 14th. That meant tomorrow was September 15th. Which also meant tomorrow was their first wedding anniversary. Or would have been. Lucy was psychologically savvy enough to realize she'd deliberately avoided thinking about that. And savvy enough to know that it had been in the back of her mind all week nonetheless.

Staring at the calendar date, her mind drifted back to her first meeting with Mike, that hot June day three months before they'd each said, "I do." She had been having trouble getting her fledgling modeling agency off the ground, and Stephie's husband, Jerry, who was a jazz aficionado and often frequented Uncle Paulie's jazz club down in the Village, recommended Mike to her.

"He's done wonders helping his uncle, and I know a half-dozen other people I've met at the club who think Mike Powell's a business genius," Jerry had said.

Stephie had seconded her husband's recommendation. "He's got a good reputation, Luce. Jerry and I met him at the club a few times. He seems like a real solid, no-nonsense type of guy with a great head on his shoulders for changing the color of a business from red to black. If you ask me, he's exactly what you need. Let's face it, you've got an incredible knack for the creative end of your business, but when it comes to the money end . . ."

She'd made an appointment to meet with him the next day. They spent all afternoon talking about the business. It was getting late. He suggested they go out for dinner to discuss the business some more. Lucy thought he'd make a pass at her that evening, and she wasn't at all averse to the prospect. Mike was refreshingly different from the men she usually dated.

However, he didn't make a pass at her. Not that night, anyway. What he did do was make it clear to her that if she wanted him to manage the financial end of her business, she was going to have to give him carte blanche to make the changes he thought were not only necessary but essential for her to turn her agency into a money-making proposition. He detailed some of the changes, drew charts on the yellow legal pad he'd brought along to the restaurant, and asked her a lot of questions—none of them personal except where it came to how she spent money. He wasn't impressed. Lucy was a little overwhelmed, but a lot impressed. Mike Powell was smart, prudent, strong-minded, confident, determined. In short, a take-charge man. He inspired confidence. By the end of that first week, Mike Powell had not only turned her whole business topsy-turvy, but her whole world.

A faint shuffle of feet reminded Lucy that her bookkeeper was still in the office. Lucy cleared her throat. "Leave the ledger, Emily. I'll deal with it tomorrow." *On my anniversary!*

"CALL ON LINE TWO, Mr. Powell," his secretary, Ann, announced over the intercom.

Mike's head jerked up from the sheet of figures he'd been unable to concentrate on all morning. His eyes shot to the phone. Was it possible . . . ? Could it be . . . ? Would she call?

His gaze shifted to the desk calendar. September 15th. Their anniversary.

He gingerly picked up the receiver. It wasn't Lucy. His disappointment was palpable. When he hung up, he picked up his pencil and began tapping it on his desk as he contemplated calling her. What would he say? "Happy Anniversary, darling"? He frowned.

The real mistake, he decided, had been moving back to the old neighborhood. What had possessed him? He knew he'd have to end up running into her. His frown deepened as he remembered their encounter at the dry cleaner's.

The pencil in his hand snapped in two just as his secretary came into the office. He gave her a distracted look as she deposited a large ledger on his desk.

Ann lingered for a moment, which wasn't like her. She was usually brisk and efficient. Now he saw that she had an odd expression on her face.

"What is it?" he asked.

Ann's gaze fell on the ledger. "The Warner Agency books."

At first her words didn't penetrate. But when they did he looked up sharply at his secretary.

"Mail? Messenger?"

Ann gave her head a little shake. "She brought them."

Mike was already out of his seat.

"She didn't wait," Ann was saying as he went flying out the door.

The elevator door was just closing as he ran into the hall. He cursed to himself as he made a beeline for the emergency stairs.

Fourteen flights. *This is crazy,* he told himself. Why was he doing this? What was he going to say to her? Nevertheless, he just picked up his speed, practically flying down each flight, determined to beat out the elevator, praying it was stopping at every floor. It was a wonder he didn't trip and end up on the bottom step in a broken heap.

When he finally made it to the lobby level, he took a couple of moments to catch his breath, smooth back his hair and straighten his tie. Then he opened the fire door and stepped into the lobby.

She was almost at the revolving door. He saw the graceful swing of her hips, the swish of her blond hair as she moved. A quick dash and he could catch up with her before she got there. Or he could just call out to her.

Suddenly, he froze. And his throat went as dry as sandpaper. A group of blue suits walked by him, obscuring his view of her for a moment. It was the moment Lucy had stopped and turned back to the lobby, hoping against hope that she'd spot Mike there; that he'd come chasing after her.

When the business group passed him, Mike's gaze shot to the revolving door. Lucy was gone.

Some happy anniversary!

3

STEPHIE BENSON SAT ACROSS from Mike's uncle in a booth at the back of his club. She'd been listening to him for a couple of minutes.

"I don't know, Paulie," she muttered dubiously when he'd finished.

Paulie sighed. "You're right. We shouldn't meddle."

Stephie grinned. "Of course, we should meddle. I just don't know if your plan will work."

Paulie chuckled. "A gal after my own heart. Pity I'm too old and you're too married."

"The real pity is that Mike and Lucy are too divorced," Stephie said wryly.

"So, what do you say?" Paulie asked expectantly. "Should I give it a whirl?"

THE GRAY-GREEN MUDPACK was just hardening on Lucy's face when her phone rang. Her heartbeat quickened. Could it be Mike? Their anniversary still had three more hours....

"Hello?" The mudpack had stiffened around her mouth so that she couldn't move her lips.

"Is that you, Lucy?"

Her mouth sagged, or would have if it could have. It wasn't Mike. It was Mike's uncle. "Yes, it's me, Uncle Paulie." She tried to sound upbeat, but couldn't pull it off. She blamed it on the mudpack.

"I got a problem, Lucy."

"Are you sick?" she asked, concern for him pushing aside her other worries. She adored Mike's uncle.

"Not exactly sick. The thing is, I've gotta go out of town. One of my boys got in a hassle in Teaneck."

"In Teaneck?"

"Yeah. You know. New Jersey."

"One of your boys?"

"Yeah. Yeah. Terry Mathers, the saxophone player. You remember Terry. He plays the club all the time. Terrific kid, but a little hotheaded. Anyway, he got himself into a jam."

"In Teaneck?"

"Yeah. Right. In Teaneck. And the thing is, I promised him I'd skip over there and . . . help him out."

"What kind of a jam?"

"It's sort of a long story, Lucy. What I'm getting at is, I've got no one to cover for me down here at the club. On top of everything else, wouldn't you know it, one of my bartenders calls in sick and the other one's getting married tomorrow so I had to give him the night off. What rotten timing, huh, Lucy? The joint is jumping. So, I was kind of hoping... Well, you are a dandy little bartender. Remember that night you and Mikey had that crazy contest? Who knew how to make the most mixed drinks?"

Lucy remembered, all right. She and Mike had made that dumb bet before going to sleep one night. It was all a joke to Mike. He'd practically been raised behind a bar. Why she'd gone along with it, she had no idea. Maybe she knew how to make a martini, a Manhattan, a screwdriver, but that was about the extent of her bartending abilities. The problem was, she loved a challenge. Especially when it came from Mike. So, at about two that morning, when she was sure Mike was asleep, she'd stolen out of bed, gotten dressed, and taken a cab down to Paulie's club. In the next three hours, he'd taught her how to mix every conceivable cocktail known to man—

and a few she was sure no human had ever actually drunk. She was back home and in bed by six that morning. That evening, down at the club, to Mike's amazement, she'd won the bet. And Paulie, the sweet dear, had never given her away.

"So, Lucy, what do you say? Will you hold down the fort for me? Just for a few hours?" There was a pleading note in Paulie's voice.

Lucy hesitated.

"I know," Paulie filled in the pause. "You're thinking, why didn't I ask Mike? I would have, but I haven't been able to get a hold of him. I've been ringing his line for hours."

"He isn't home?" Lucy asked deflatedly. Where was he? Out on a date? With that snooty Royce? Or a Royce look-alike? On their anniversary, of all nights? The bastard. The bum. And to think she was just sitting around her apartment, a stupid mudpack on her face, feeling sorry for herself, sorry for everything.

"Okay, damn it," she said vehemently. "Sure. Why not? It'll be fun. Who knows? Maybe I'll even meet some tall, dark, handsome stranger."

On the other end of the line, Paulie grinned. "Hey, who knows? Anything's possible, Lucy."

"COME ON, UNCLE PAULIE. I've got a pile of work staring me in the face. I'll be lucky if I get this stuff taken care of by morning."

"Mikey, how often do I ask you a favor?" Paulie's voice held just the right note of disappointment and reproval.

"Who did you say this guy was?" Mike's eyes strayed to the stack of papers he'd carted home from the office hours ago. He hadn't been able to deal with a single report even though he'd vowed he wasn't going to just sit around moping all night. After all, it wasn't actually an anniversary if you weren't even married anymore. Was it?

"Terry. Terry Mathers. You know. Beard, long hair—"

"Half of your musicians have beards and long hair."

"He plays the sax. I've known him since he was knee-high."

"Knee-high?"

"You know what I mean, Mikey. He's been playing at the club for years, off and on. The kid's got a good heart, Mikey. And you know me."

Mike smiled. "Yeah, I know you, Uncle Paulie." He sighed, thinking to himself that maybe being down at the club, around a crowd of people, might not be such a bad idea. He'd be so busy mixing drinks, he wouldn't have time to think about Lucy. Or go on cursing himself for not chasing after her that afternoon in the lobby of his office building. "Two hours?"

"Give or take a couple of minutes."

"It's been a long time since I've tended bar for you, Uncle Paulie. I'm not sure—"

"Hey, you came pretty close to beating Lucy out on that bet a few months back," Paulie reminded him.

As if Mike needed reminding. He laughed. So did Paulie. "How could I not let her win after all the trouble she went to?" Mike said, smiling. "It was all I could do to keep a straight face, watching her mix all those cocktails like a pro. She really thought I was in dreamland when she snuck off in the middle of the night. Like I didn't know what she had up her sleeve."

"I never breathed a word, did I, Mikey?"

"No, Uncle Paulie. You never did," he said wistfully. "And neither did I."

"That's right, Mike. You never did." And it was no secret to either uncle or nephew as to why.

JEFF ALTON, ONE OF THE two bartenders at the Bennett Street Club & Grill was dumbfounded. "You're kidding, Paulie.

We've got a packed house and you want me and Nick to take the rest of the night off?"

"That's right, kid," Paulie said, checking his watch. "And step on it."

"You can't handle the bar on your own, Paulie. It's crazy."

"Oh, I'm heading out, too."

"What? Man, have you flipped or something?"

Paulie chuckled. "I flipped way before your time, kid. Don't worry. I've got a pair of top-notch replacements coming in. They're gonna do a bang-up job, believe me."

Jeff narrowed his gaze on his boss. "Hey, look, Paulie, if you're not happy with my work or you've got a beef . . ."

Paulie patted his employee's back. "It's nothing of the sort. Just a one-night stand for a couple of kids I happen to be crazy about. Well, actually I'm hoping it'll be more than just a one-night stand. But I promise you, your job is as secure as Fort Knox."

"Two kids you're crazy about, huh?" The bartender grinned. "You wily old coot. Aren't you too old to be playing matchmaker?"

Paulie laughed. "Kid, the hell of it is, I'm too old to be doing much of anything else."

"WHY, LUCY, DON'T YOU look pretty tonight," Eunice Blanford said enthusiastically as she and her friend Clara Ponds encountered their upstairs neighbor in the lobby of their apartment building.

"Very nice," Clara muttered, a touch of disapproval in her voice. The bright red jersey dress was rather skimpy and a bit too formfitting for her liking.

"I believe your Cynthia wore something similar to Bill's birthday party last month," Eunice added.

Clara frowned. "She wore no such thing." Clara did have the good grace to mutter an apology to Lucy for her rude response.

Lucy smiled. She rather liked the two old women even though they could both prove trying at times—Clara, because of her cynicism and critical eye; Eunice, because of her overabundant enthusiasm and inquisitiveness. Shortly after she and Mike had moved into the building and gotten corralled by the elderly twosome into having "a spot of afternoon tea" with them, Mike had affectionately dubbed them The Odd Couple.

"Isn't it rather late to be going out, Lucy?" Clara remarked, having recovered from her faux pas.

"Well . . ." Lucy started, but Eunice cut her off.

"Do you have a date, dear?"

"Not exactly."

"Well, of course it's none of our business, is it, Clara. Still, what with all the crime you see on the television and read about in the papers, it's our firm opinion that one—especially one of the female persuasion—shouldn't be out alone at night."

"I don't agree, Eunice," Clara stated firmly.

Eunice looked aghast. "Of course, you agree, Clara."

"What I was going to say before I was so rudely interrupted was that I don't agree that it isn't any of our business," Clara said haughtily. "As responsible citizens I think we have to advise innocent young women—"

"Just like on that news show we were watching the other night," Eunice interrupted. "'20/20'— Or was it '42 Hours'?"

Lucy surreptitiously checked her watch. She'd promised Paulie she'd be down at the club by nine. And it had taken her nearly fifteen minutes just to get that mudpack off her face. She tried to break in on the two women and explain she was in a hurry, but as Lucy knew from numerous past experiences, it was a feat to get a word in edgewise with this loquacious duo.

Lucy made a stab at it. "Excuse me—"

"'48 Hours,'" Clara corrected, ignoring Lucy. "You haven't once stayed awake for '20/20,' Eunice. I always have to shake you because you start to snore a good ten minutes before the show even starts."

"That isn't true. I might take a catnap every now and then—"

"I've never heard a cat snore," Clara snickered.

"How would you know whether or not a cat snores," Eunice retorted. "You abhor cats. And dogs. And you know, they do say a house isn't a home without a pet."

Lucy wondered if she could just sneak around the pair, unobserved, and make her escape. But Eunice gripped her arm as she took a sidestep. "What do you think, dear?"

"Think? I think . . . I really have to—"

"This is a ridiculous conversation," Clara said sharply. Lucy had lost track of the conversation.

"And why is it ridiculous?" Eunice countered, her grip still firm on Lucy's arm.

"Because pets are not allowed in this building," Clara replied, a note of triumph in her voice.

"That's true," Lucy said, trying to use this as an opening to say that she really was in a hurry. "I'm afraid—"

Eunice gripped her arm even tighter. "Oh, dear, don't tell me you're afraid of dogs. Or is it cats?"

Lucy rolled her eyes. "No, no. You don't understand."

"I know your husband was very fond of animals," Eunice said. "Don't you remember, Clara? We saw him playing with that little boy and his dog in the park just a few months ago." She eyed Lucy closely. "A pet might have helped, you know."

"Oh, for heaven's sake, Eunice," Clara said, exasperated. "There's a world of difference between a mangy animal and a child. Not that I, for one, have ever adhered to the ridiculous notion that couples should have a child to try to hold a failing marriage together."

Lucy felt a wave of melancholy, thinking about how, only a month before their final blowup, she and Mike had talked about having a baby. Not to hold their failing marriage together; neither of them had thought it was failing. Despite their blowups. Until that last one . . .

It took a moment for Lucy to realize the two women had finally stopped jabbering. Instead, they were staring straight at her, both of them looking duly chastened.

"We do go on so, sometimes," Clara muttered.

Eunice smiled weakly. "We weren't really talking about *your* failed marriage . . . in particular."

Clara frowned at her friend. "Come, Eunice."

"It's just . . . Well, we did think the two of you made such a nice . . ."

"Come, Eunice," Clara repeated sharply, marching into the elevator.

"Yes, Clara." As Eunice stepped into the elevator she gave Lucy a wilted smile.

"Honestly, Eunice," Clara scolded as the elevator doors started to close.

"I was only suggesting to Lucy that a pet—mind you, I said pet, not baby—has a way of . . . of livening things up around a house."

"Things were livened up enough at the Powells'—"

The doors slid shut on Clara's summation.

PAULIE FINISHED SERVING his customer a beer and rushed out from the bar to meet Lucy, who'd had to thread her way through the crowd. Over the din of voices, a jazz combo was just warming up. It was Friday night and Paulie was right: The joint was jumping.

"You look like dynamite, kid," Paul said, bussing Lucy's cheek and tying an apron around her waist at the same time. "The place is all yours. I've got to rush."

Lucy anxiously searched the area for a second bartender. There wasn't one. She stopped short. "You don't mean 'all mine' literally, Paulie."

"Don't worry about a thing. I've got someone due in to help you any minute now." Any minute was right, Paulie was thinking. And if Mikey showed up before he got out of there, he knew both his nephew and his nephew's ex-wife would have his head.

"Two beers, a Scotch on the rocks and a Bloody Mary, light on the Tabasco sauce," Darlene, one of the old-time waitresses at the club, barked practically in Lucy's ear.

Paulie gave her back a pat that was more a little nudge and disappeared into the crowd. Lucy sighed and reluctantly stepped behind the bar.

A couple of minutes later, the bottle of Tabasco was poised in Lucy's hand right over the Bloody Mary when someone on the other side of the bar caught her eye. Her mouth dropped open. A good twenty drops of the fiery liquid slipped into the drink as Lucy stared at her ex-husband.

"What are you doing here?" she demanded, looking around to see who he was with. How could he bring a date here? And on their anniversary, no less. The man had a heart of stone. That's all there was to it.

"That sneaky no-account character," Mike mumbled, his brows knitting together in a frown.

"Your date?" Lucy asked, taken aback.

Mike looked at her like she was nuts. "What date?"

"What sneaky no-account character?"

"Paulie."

Lucy's eyes widened. "Paulie?" No sooner had the name left her lips than her eyes narrowed. Okay, so she was a little slow on the uptake. Mike's unexpected appearance had caught her by surprise. "That sneaky no-account character," she echoed.

Darlene hurried over to the bar. "Hi ya, Mike. Long time no see." She gave him a knowing wink, then glanced at the drinks in front of Lucy. "These all set?"

Lucy nodded dumbly, putting down the bottle of Tabasco. Darlene scooped up the overdosed Bloody Mary along with the rest of the order, placed the drinks on her tray and scooted off.

Before either Lucy or Mike got to say another word, two more waitresses appeared, rattling off their drink orders rapid-fire. Shaking his head, Mike slid behind the bar. They both started filling the orders, muttering to themselves as they did.

A couple of hectic minutes had passed when a bruiser of a fellow, his face almost a beet red, loomed over Lucy from across the bar. "Hey, you the one that mixed that Bloody Mary?" he demanded in a low raspy voice charged with menace.

Lucy, who was trying to remember whether brandy went into a White Russian, gave him a blank look. "What?"

"The Bloody Mary that just about burned my throat raw. Was it a joke or something?" he roared, his face getting even redder if that was possible. "Honey, I ain't laughing!"

"Look, I don't . . ."

Mike hurried over. "You got a problem?" he asked the customer evenly.

"A problem? Yeah, I got a problem. I ordered a Bloody Mary light on the Tabasco, and instead I got straight Tabasco with a little Bloody Mary thrown in. My girl almost had to ring 911 for the fire department."

"She didn't make that Bloody Mary. I did," Mike lied. "I'm sorry about the Tabasco. Something else must have caught my eye while I was making the drink. Can I make it up to you by picking up your bar tab for the evening? For you and your girl."

The angry customer, already geared up for a fight, was caught off guard. "I got six people in my party."

"No problem," Mike said amiably.

The customer cleared his throat. "I guess— Hell, anyone can make a mistake. Sure. Sure, that's real nice of you."

"And how about you give me another chance on that Bloody Mary?" Mike offered.

"Skip the Tabasco altogether this time."

Mike smiled. "You got it."

After the customer sauntered off, Lucy gave Mike a sheepish smile. "You know very well that I made that Bloody Mary. You didn't have to take the rap."

"I know," Mike said cautiously. He worried Lucy might turn around and accuse him of thinking she couldn't have handled the guy on her own.

She wasn't thinking anything of the sort. Seeing Mike tonight, she was gripped by nostalgia. He was wearing a blue-and-white pin-striped button-down shirt and pleated gray slacks that accented his trimness. He looked neat, well-groomed, and terrific. Aware that he was staring at her expectantly for some kind of response, she murmured, "Thanks, Mike. The guy did get me a bit rattled."

Their gazes met and held for a beat. But the drink orders were piling up and the waitresses were getting restless.

For the next two hours Mike and Lucy raced around the bar, whipping up drinks, hardly saying much more than, "That one gets an olive," or, "We're running short on limes," to each other.

Darlene came over at around eleven to tell them she'd just heard from Paulie. With a sheepish smile, she announced that he wasn't going to be able to make it back from "Teaneck" tonight, and could they close up shop for him.

The news didn't come as a surprise to either Lucy or Mike.

By one that morning, the club had begun to empty. "Hey, why don't you two take a break," Darlene suggested, "and I'll man the fort for a while. Mindy's covering my section. If you want, I can even close up tonight if you don't get a second wind."

Neither of them made a peep of protest about taking a break. They were both beat. As Lucy headed over to a quiet corner table, Mike hung back for a minute, snatching up a bottle of champagne and a couple of goblets.

Lucy didn't say a word as Mike popped the cork and poured them each a drink. He hesitated for a moment before tapping her glass and offering up a toast. Lucy was afraid if he said happy anniversary, she might actually start blubbering. She was in a funny mood. Not ha-ha funny. More strange funny. Discombobulated.

His glass clinked with hers. "Here's lookin' at you, kid."

Lucy smiled. "You always did do a great Bogart."

Suddenly, they were silent, both remembering other Bogart impressions of Mike's. Some very sexy impressions. When she was wrapped around him in their queen-size bed...

They each took a large swallow of champagne. Lucy set hers down, cupping it in both hands. "You have a devious uncle, Mike."

"Very devious." He took another swallow of champagne and set his glass down, too.

"He told me you were out and I was the only one he could turn to," Lucy said.

"I wasn't out." Mike glanced over at the combo. They were playing a slow, bluesy number.

Lucy's eyes followed his gaze. "They're good."

A slow smile curved Mike's lips. "Do you think the sax player compares to Terry Whatever His Name Was?"

"The Terry who's in trouble in Teaneck?" Lucy laughed. "Where was my head?"

Mike laughed, too. "Hey, I fell for the same pitch. We both got taken in by the old devil."

Lucy's smile faded. "I suppose he meant well." She watched the bubbles in her champagne pop.

"I guess he was hoping..." Mike let the sentence trail off.

"Silly man," Lucy muttered, conscious of her heartbeat.

Neither of them knew what to say next. Mike made a stab at it.

"That's some dress, Lucy."

"Does that mean you like it or you don't?"

He smiled. "I like what you do for it."

Lucy actually flushed. Mike Powell was not given to such provocative compliments. She was glad the club was dimly lit. Her eyes strayed to the jazz combo. "They're good." She flushed even more, realizing she'd already said that.

Mike merely nodded. Another lull fell.

"Want to dance?" Mike asked hesitantly. "For old times' sake."

Lucy ran the tip of her tongue over her dry lips. A little tremor zigzagged down her spine. She worried that her palms might be sweaty.

"If you'd rather not..."

She jumped up. "No, no. I mean yes. Yes, let's dance." She took in a breath. "For... old times' sake."

As they started for the dance floor, Mike was filled with misgivings. He was a lousy dancer. Except for that one time.... Again that "anniversary" dance flashed through his mind. Well, this was their real anniversary. In an unreal sort of way. Maybe he'd rise to the occasion. With that thought and another glance at his ex-wife in that sexy fire-engine-red dress, it was Mike's turn to flush. He might "rise" to the occasion, all right. However, dancing was another matter altogether.

No sooner had they got to the dance floor, Mike slipping his arm around Lucy's slender waist, Lucy's arm encircling Mike's shoulders, when the music stopped and the piano player announced a ten-minute break.

Couples ambled off the floor. Mike and Lucy stood there motionless, almost but not quite cheek to cheek, their hearts racing. Seconds passed as they continued holding each other in a half-dance position, half embrace.

"Funny, being together like this . . . on our anniversary," Mike murmured.

A whisper of a smile curved Lucy's lips. "I bet Uncle Paulie's having a chuckle in 'Teaneck'."

Oblivious to the stares of patrons and employees alike at the Bennett Street Club, the pair still hadn't budged from the dance floor.

"I don't think Uncle Paulie's ever been to Teaneck in his life."

Lucy grinned. "No, I think you're right."

"Lucy?" Suddenly Mike's voice was very serious.

Lucy held her breath. "Yes?"

"Lucy, do you . . . ?"

"Yes . . ."

Mike wasn't sure whether her last yes was a question or a response. Neither was Lucy.

He inhaled sharply. So did she. Their cheeks were touching now. And he was stroking her back. The rhythm of his touch stirred her, stirred so many memories. Her knees felt weak.

"Mike?"

"Yes?"

"The music's...stopped." She tilted her head back and met his gaze.

"I don't think it . . . started."

"Oh."

Her lips were still parted when he leaned closer and kissed her. They got a round of applause. Embarrassed, aroused, excited beyond reason, their mouths separated and they literally ran out of the club.

Giddily, they kissed again in the cab a couple of minutes later. Mike's hand was cruising down her thigh and Lucy kept having to catch her breath, each intake of air sending a plume of sensation through her body.

Lucy's mind was whirling. *What am I doing? This is crazy. This man's my ex-husband. We're divorced!* Nevertheless, she couldn't recall ever feeling this kind of urgency, this intensity of desire. She was bursting with it. If the damn cab didn't pull up in front of the Harkness Towers soon, public shame be damned, she might have to seduce Mike right here in this cab.

Mike was feeling just as crazy with desire. He didn't know what had come over him. Propriety was usually a top priority with him. He didn't go in for public displays of affection. He was a very private person. And this woman he was stroking and caressing in this public vehicle was his ex-wife.

The cab stopped at a red light. Another car pulled up beside them. Lucy and Mike drew apart, trying to regain a modicum of composure.

"It's a nice night," she said inanely, smoothing down her dress, thinking, *I can't let this happen. It's not going to change anything. It's just lust. . . .*

"Yes," Mike agreed earnestly, thinking, *If I let this go any further, we'll both be sorry in the morning. The morning? What am I thinking? Spend the night? With my ex-wife? In my ex-bed?*

The cab pulled out and turned left. Lucy lurched against Mike. She stayed put. A second later their lips were wedded. They kissed with even greater fervor, as Mike's hand, with a will all its own, slipping wantonly beneath the hem of Lucy's dress, cupping her knee, edging up to her thigh.

"Did you say Harkness Towers on Central Park West?" the cabbie asked, glancing back at them.

Completely embarrassed and more than a little dazed, they leaped apart, nodding mutely to the driver.

The cabbie, an older man who, ironically, bore an uncanny resemblance to Uncle Paulie, winked. "We're here."

4

"I'LL JUST...WALK YOU inside," Mike muttered as Lucy's hand gripped the door handle of the cab.

"Oh...thanks. That would be...nice," she mumbled, smoothing down the hem of her dress as she opened the door.

The cabbie caught Mike's eye as Mike was about to head out of the cab after Lucy. "You want I should wait for ya?"

Mike's eyes were on Lucy's swaying hips as she headed toward the apartment building. He gave a surreptitious shake of his head and slipped the cabbie a twenty from his billfold.

"Keep the change," Mike said, not even paying attention to what the meter read. For once he didn't stop to calculate what he considered an appropriate fifteen-percent tip.

The cabbie grinned as he palmed the twenty. Nothing wrong with a twelve-buck tip on a slow night. "You have yourself a nice night, buddy."

THEY CROSSED THE LOBBY together, deliberately not touching, desperately trying to put things into some kind of perspective, or failing that, to at least get a grip on their libidos.

Lucy's fingers were trembling as she pushed the Up button for the elevator. They stood there, waiting, not speaking a word, still not touching. Finally the doors slid open. Lucy hesitated for a moment. She turned to Mike.

"I'll just...see you upstairs," he said huskily.

"Oh...Thanks." Her voice was breathy.

They stepped inside the elevator. When their shoulders brushed, they quickly moved apart. Like boxers in a ring, they stood in opposite corners of the elevator—all the while sneaking glances, sizing each other up.

There ought to be a law against a woman looking this desirable, Mike was thinking, as he took in his ex-wife's flawless skin, her blond hair falling in careless, lustrous waves down around her milky-white shoulders. And those full, alluring lips. It was going to take every ounce of his willpower to keep from falling prey to them again. He had to get control over himself. It was sheer madness. Where would it lead? As if he didn't know. The real question was, where would it lead after that? She'd wanted the divorce. And he'd gone along with it willingly. Oil and water, oil and water, oil and water. Sure, there'd been some fun in the shaking, as Uncle Paulie had so inimitably put it; but then he and Lucy had gotten too shook-up. Mike's gaze shifted to the floor numbers over the doors, lighting up in sequence as the elevator rose. As each number lit up, Mike saw them as flashing warning signs that spelled, Watch Out.

Lucy stood motionless in the elevator, trying to fight her overwhelming attraction to her ex-husband. Her gaze met his for an instant before they both looked away. She could lose herself in his eyes, in his arms. Fierce electric attraction mingled with nervous tension. Passion, recklessly ignited, had gotten her into trouble before—with the very man who was now standing beside her in the elevator. *I can't let this happen. I won't.*

The elevator came to a stop at the fifteenth floor. The doors slid open. Neither moved. Now the doors were wide open. Lucy and Mike stared into the hallway, rooted to the spot. The doors started to close.

When they closed fully, the two of them still standing there in the elevator, Lucy murmured an "oh" that was half a cry of alarm, half something else altogether.

"Lucy. . ." Her name was a mere whisper of desire on his lips.

The hell with reason, Mike thought. *The hell with common sense,* Lucy thought. They hesitated for the briefest instant before they hurtled against each other like they were magnetized. Their lips met, then their mouths opened, their bodies locking together in an ardent embrace. He lifted her inches off the floor, pressed her up against the wall of the elevator, deepening their kiss.

"Lucy. Oh, Lucy."

"Mike, Mike . . ."

Impatiently, they clawed at each other's clothing.

"Oh, Lucy. You feel so good, so soft, so silky," he murmured huskily into her hair, against her neck, into her cleavage. He found the zipper at the side of her dress and drew it down. She wore no bra. Her lush breasts were fully exposed. Mike let out a cry of delight as he cupped them, burying his face between them.

Lucy clung to him, her knees wobbly. She'd pulled his shirt out of his trousers, her hands cruising up his smooth, muscular back. Then she slid one hand between them, unfastening his belt buckle with eager, trembling fingers.

Her dress was hiked up and Mike was busy slipping her red silk panties down over her hips as Lucy worked furiously at the button closure on his waistband. The button popped off. The elevator lurched just as she finished lowering his zipper.

"Oh, no. We're moving!" she cried. "Someone must have pressed for the elevator."

Mike's trousers dropped around his ankles as he madly pressed the button for fifteen, then the Open button, so they could make their escape and avert almost certain humiliation. Too late. The elevator kept moving down. In her panic, Lucy tried to zip her dress closed only to jam the zipper halfway up. And her panties. Where were her panties?

Under Mike's shoe. She bent to retrieve them, nudging Mike out of the way. With his trousers down around his ankles, his balance wasn't the best. He started to topple backward. Lucy tried to grab him to prevent him from falling. Momentum and everything else was against her. She went toppling after him.

"Oh, Mike, Mike," she cried, struggling to her feet. "Do something."

He managed to pull his pants back on and get them zipped and then get to his feet. Meanwhile Lucy attacked the zipper of her dress again, miraculously unjamming it and zipping it up just as the elevator door opened onto the fifth floor.

A young man dressed in a tux stepped into the elevator, casting the disheveled but basically dressed pair a curious glance.

"Down?" the new arrival asked, his finger poised on the button.

Mike nodded. Lucy shook her head. They reversed their gestures.

The young man merely smiled and pressed the Down button. A few seconds later, the doors of the elevator opened onto the lobby. The young man whistled as he stepped out.

Once again, Lucy and Mike stood there, frozen.

"I should . . . go," Mike said as the doors started to close. His voice was strained.

"Yes. I suppose . . ." Lucy murmured, staring down at the button that had popped from Mike's trousers.

The doors continued to close. Neither of them moved. Neither did the elevator, even as the doors shut fully. One of them was going to have to press a button or they would stand there waiting for someone else to come along.

Mike stepped closer to the panel. All he had to do was press the button that read lobby and he was out of there. Slowly, he lifted his hand.

Go on, Mike. Play it safe. Play it smart. Don't be a jerk. Don't go looking for trouble.

Lucy stared fixedly at Mike's hand. She held her breath, trying to convince herself she truly did want him to press lobby and not 15. *Liar, liar, hair's on fire....*

With his finger poised by the lobby button but not quite touching it, he glanced back at her. In that single shared look, they both felt as if their hearts would crush. His hand rose. He pressed 15 without even looking.

They were still kissing when the elevator reached their floor. This time they managed to stay dressed until Lucy got the door of the apartment open and they stepped inside the dark, inviting, familiar space. They stripped in the blackness, both of them naked by the time they got to their bedroom. *Their* bedroom. Only it wasn't theirs anymore. It was Lucy's. Mike forced that thought aside as they fell together, embracing, onto the queen-size bed.

"I've never wanted you so much," he admitted, kissing her throat, her jaw, her mouth.

Lucy fit herself tightly against him. *Such a good fit,* she thought. *A perfect fit.*

They stroked and caressed each other, touching, tasting, rediscovering, renewing memories. Lucy's moans of pleasure warmed Mike to the bones.

"Oh, Mike, this isn't wrong, is it?" she whispered. "We won't be sorry, will we?"

"No, no," Mike said vehemently—a lie almost as smooth as Lucy's skin. They were bound to be sorry. They both knew it. For once, Mike was determined to live for the moment. Hadn't that been one of Lucy's complaints when they were married? That he'd been too restrained, took everything too seriously, considered and weighed every little move he made?

He slid his hands down her bare back, gently massaging the muscles. She loved to be massaged.

Breathing raggedly, she sought his lips with hers as her hand snaked down between their bodies, curling around him. Now it was Mike's turn to moan with delight.

His massage grew more erotic as his hands moved over her firm, smooth buttocks, down the backs of her slender, muscular thighs. His lips trailed her high cheekbones, her swan's neck, her luscious breasts. He whispered her name over and over. "Lucy, Lucy, Lucy..."

When he slid on top of her, her legs parted, her fingers twining in his dark brown hair. A jolt of lightning quivered down her spine. A few months ago, she'd made love with this very same man and it was all perfectly natural and simple. Now, it was illicit. And that added an extra dimension, a new excitement, a little fear, too.

"Lucy, it's been so long...."

She arched up into him. "Mike. Oh, Mike. I've missed this," she confessed, wanting to feel him grind into her, fill her with his rhythmic thrusts as he'd done so many nights in the past. But tonight Mike's imagination was sparked as it had never been before. He kept shifting their positions—even when she protested, thinking nothing could be better than the one they'd already found. But it was better. Better, better, best.

"Oh, yes. Oh, Mike. That feels ... perfect," she cried feverishly. Still he broke the rhythm to suckle and fondle her until she was writhing, certain she would erupt, explode.

When, at last, he began driving into her, Lucy matched his hot, insatiable thrusts, both of them breathless, swept along in an ever-escalating crescendo, each of them trying to memorize every incredible sensation because they both knew it might never happen again.

When their lovemaking ended, neither of them knew what to say. She lay against him as he held her close, feeling the tension like sweat coming through their pores.

She lifted her head. "Mike."

His stomach knotted. "Do you want me to leave?"

His question jolted her. "It's awfully late."

"Right," he said. "I should get going."

"No. I mean... It's so late you might as well... wait ... for ... morning."

"That's true. It is ... almost morning anyway."

"Right."

"So, I might as well ..." Mike murmured.

"You might as well ..." Lucy agreed.

Within minutes, Mike was fast asleep. Lucy shut her eyes, hoping to doze off, too, but had no such luck. A mix of guilt, carnal desire and confusion made sleep impossible. Taking care not to wake Mike, she slipped out of bed, padded across the room and stood by the window, drawing the curtain aside. She always loved the city when the streets were almost empty, when just a few lights in other buildings on the Upper East Side sparkled across the dark expanse of Central Park.

She looked back at Mike as he rolled over, his movement dislodging the light summer blanket. He lay there naked and she let her gaze drift unabashedly down his strong, lean body. It was a mistake, because she wanted him again. This sudden greediness of her lust surprised and alarmed her.

She turned away, telling herself over and over again that they'd divorced for all the right reasons. It wasn't that he was in the wrong or that she was. They just had different metabolisms, different outlooks on life, different appetites. Except when it came to sex. There, their appetites were right in tune. Deliciously in tune.

She crawled back into bed and snuggled against him. He stirred.

"Are you asleep?" she whispered.

"Mmm."

"Are you dreaming?"

"Mmm."

Ever so lightly, she kissed his lips. "Is it a good dream?"

"The best," he murmured sleepily, his hand slipping between her thighs.

A soft moan escaped her lips. His hand slipped higher. She gave another moan.

"Come into my dream," he murmured, drawing her to him.

"Where are we?"

"A tropical paradise. Swaying palm trees. Ocean breezes. Warm white sand."

"You hate sand."

"Shh. We're lying together on a blanket, all golden and naked."

"A nude beach?"

"No, no. Our own private Eden, silly."

Lucy sighed. "This is a nice dream, Mike."

"It gets better." His hand drifted higher still. "Can you feel the delicious warmth of the sun?"

"Oh, I feel it. I definitely feel it." She gasped as his fingers began a feathery massage that made all her muscles contract, and made goose bumps spring up over her whole body.

"And the whoosh of the waves," he whispered as his fingers shifted into a rhythmic assault.

"Oh, if this is a dream, don't wake me, Mike."

Then it was no longer his fingers, but his mouth, and then his tongue sending incendiary shock waves of ecstasy through her. She cried out his name, as she felt herself going over the edge, dissolving into a long spasm of rapture.

When she finally managed to catch her breath, she climbed on top of him. His arms encircled her, drawing her up a little higher. Her hand guided him inside her.

The instant he felt himself engulfed by her heat, the connection was electric. Mike clasped her fiercely against him.

As he climaxed she watched the magic of the moment on his face, his lips parted, head flung back, muscles taut. It was almost as erotic watching him as it was to reach climax herself. Which she did again just moments later.

"You can invite me into your dreams anytime," she whispered afterward, as they curled up against each other.

"Do you mean that, Lucy?"

He felt her stiffen. He stiffened in response. "Sorry," he said softly. "I shouldn't have put you on the spot."

"We'd better get some sleep."

"Right. It's almost dawn. A little sleep is just what we need."

They did finally doze off, but it took a lot of effort on both their parts.

MIKE ROSE AT NINE the next morning, despite having had only a couple of hours of sleep at the most. He always woke at nine on Saturdays and keeping to a routine was important to him. He slipped quietly out of the bedroom so as not to wake Lucy, who always enjoyed sleeping late, whether it was on the weekend or on a workday. He found himself remembering their endless arguments when she would balk at his efforts to waken her so she wouldn't be late for work. Lucy would argue that being late was one of the privileges that came with being the boss. Mike disagreed, his philosophy being that the boss was the one who should set an example for the employees by arriving not only on time, but early. One of the many things they hadn't seen eye-to-eye on.

He gathered up his clothes that led in a trail from the bedroom to the front entry, dressing as he made his way to the door. His hand was on the doorknob when he was startled by Lucy's voice.

"You're leaving?"

She stood at the open doorway of the bedroom, groggy, her hair disheveled, naked, save for a cotton robe slung over her arm. To Mike she had never looked more breathtakingly beautiful. "No. I was just . . . I was going to run over to the bakery for some croissants and coffee."

"I could . . . cook some eggs or something."

He frowned, remembering the last time she'd cooked eggs and they'd landed in his face.

Lucy remembered, too. "Actually, I've given up eggs. Too high in cholesterol." She slipped on her robe, suddenly feeling chilled.

"Probably a smart idea," Mike mumbled.

"I could make us something else, though." She knew how much Mike liked a home-cooked meal. Growing up, he'd eaten most of his meals at Uncle Paulie's club. The problem was, she hated to cook. She also hated the mundane chore of grocery shopping, so there never was much in the fridge. She was great at making reservations, though.

There'd been plenty of times in the not-so-distant past when Mike would have taken Lucy up on her offer to make breakfast, even though he knew cooking wasn't her thing. He'd kept on hoping that she'd get to enjoy it. At first, he'd offered to help her with the cooking, but she'd said he made her nervous around the kitchen. He was too meticulous, too precise, too helpful.

He smiled at her. "I'm in the mood for croissants." He knew they were Lucy's favorite. "Almond or chocolate?"

"Almond."

He nodded.

"Well, maybe chocolate," she said.

He waited.

She frowned. "I don't know. What are you going to have?"

He sighed. Typical Lucy. She never could make up her mind. Which was one of the reasons he'd hated their eating out so much. First she'd have the waiter or waitress describe a good dozen selections from the menu, asking detailed questions, then she'd spend agonizing minutes debating, ordering, changing her mind, changing it back. Suffering through Lucy ordering a meal invariably gave him a headache—as well as the poor wait person taking her order.

Lucy's frown deepened. "Oh, I know what you're thinking."

Mike knew that she knew. Lucy could invariably read his mind. But he wanted to avoid an argument. It was no way to end one of the high points of his life. And making love with Lucy last night had definitely been a high point.

"I was thinking that I'd get a couple of each and then you could have half chocolate, half almond," he lied, knowing she knew he was lying and hoping she'd let him get away with it.

She did. She didn't want to argue, either. "A perfect solution."

They shared a knowing smile.

MIKE STARTED TO WHISTLE a happy little tune as he stepped into the elevator. He was still whistling as the doors slid open one floor below.

Clara Ponds and Eunice Blanford always did their grocery shopping on Saturday mornings. As they entered the elevator, the two women gave Mike startled looks.

"Why, what a nice surprise!" Eunice said a moment or two after the shock of seeing Lucy's ex-husband wore off.

Clara eyed him curiously and a bit warily. One never knew about ex-husbands, she thought. The tabloids always printed simply dreadful things about angry exes coming back to do their wives in. What if he'd been lurking in the shadows last night and spotted her going out for the evening, wearing that skimpy, provocative dress? Really, how could Eunice have thought Cynthia's dress was anything like the one Lucy had been wearing? It wasn't at all.

Clara gave Michael a wary look. What if he had spied Lucy meeting another man last night? What if Lucy had even brought the man back to her apartment for an assignation? Mike could have gone berserk with jealousy, used his old key to let himself in, caught the unsuspecting pair right in the act.... What if Lucy and some strange man were lying up there in her bedroom this very moment? Dead.

A little gasp escaped Clara's lips.

"Are you all right, dear?" Eunice asked with concern.

"You do look a bit pale, Mrs. Ponds," Mike said sympathetically.

Clara shook her head, muttering that she was just fine, and telling herself that if Mike had killed Lucy and her lover, surely he wouldn't have been whistling gaily in the elevator. He wouldn't even be in the elevator—someone might see him. Someone *had* seen him. Surely, he'd be the first one the police would suspect, anyway. And if there were eye witnesses to his having been on the scene— No, he might be a murderer, but he was also an accountant. And accountants were too shrewd to do anything that dumb.

Of course, Clara considered, the man could be quite mad. In his warped state of mind he might not even think he'd done anything wrong. Or he might not even remember. She stepped farther away from Mike.

"Really, Mrs. Ponds, you don't look well," Mike said, stepping closer to her, his hand moving to her arm.

Clara let out a sharp cry at his touch. Mike immediately backed off, giving her a puzzled look.

Eunice, too, was baffled by her friend's behavior. What had gotten into Clara? Was she such a prude as to object to an ex-husband spending a night with his ex-wife? Eunice thought it very romantic. She even thought this could be the start of a reconciliation between the pair. In her opinion, Lucy and Mike belonged together.

Clara gripped Eunice's arm as the elevator doors opened and practically dragged her companion out, hurrying her across the lobby to the street. Mike wore a bemused expression as he watched them rush off.

"I TELL YOU, IT'S POSSIBLE," Clara argued, glancing nervously over her shoulder as they started down the street toward the grocery store. She spotted Mike exiting the building, and was relieved to see that he turned in the other direction.

"Must you think the worst, Clara?" Eunice countered.

"I'm a realist. I don't look at life through rose-colored glasses like you do, Eunice. You refuse to recognize that people can have a dark side."

"Mike Powell? He's such a nice, quiet, well-mannered young man," Eunice argued. "If anyone was likely to fly off the handle and do something . . . drastic, it would have been Lucy. She's the short-tempered one. Not that I'm saying Lucy would ever do something *that* drastic."

"It's the quiet ones you have to watch out for," Clara said forebodingly.

Eunice gave her companion's words careful thought. Then she came to a halt. "There's only one thing to do."

"Call the police?"

"No. Go right up to Lucy's apartment and see if she's all right." Eunice started to turn around but then spun back, gripping Clara's arm. "It's him. He's going back into the building."

Clara pressed her hand to her chest. "Oh, dear. That's not good."

"What do you mean?" Eunice asked anxiously.

"He might have left something incriminating behind."

"Or maybe he didn't finish the...deed?" Eunice murmured. "He was carrying a bag."

"It could be a weapon. A gun. A knife. Maybe poison," Clara said.

They pretended to avidly study a store window that sold fishing supplies until Mike disappeared into the building. Then they hurried back down the street after him.

5

"LUCY, I'M BACK!" Mike called out as he stepped into the apartment. Lucy, dressed in white shorts and a bright-pink T-shirt, stuck her head out of the bathroom, toothbrush in hand. "Be out in a jiff."

A "jiff" to Lucy could be anywhere from a half hour to an hour. The coffee would get cold. So would the fresh-from-the oven croissants. Lucy wouldn't care. She'd just pop everything into the microwave.

He knelt down and picked up her panties and her dress off the floor in the hallway. He smiled. In the past, they'd argued about Lucy always leaving all her things lying about. But last night he'd been as eager as she was to just drop his clothes and let them fall where they might.

He slid her panties into his slacks pocket, intending to drop them in the hamper in the bathroom for her after she came out. As he hung her red dress on a hanger from the hall closet he caught sight of a well-known designer label. His smile drooped. The dress had to have cost Lucy a fortune. A lot of good all his lectures about her needing to budget her money and live within her means had done him. Okay, so it was her own business now. And all her own money. She hadn't asked for a dime from him after they'd split up. That was the main reason they'd been able to get the divorce so quickly. No issues to haggle over, nothing to contest. Funny, they'd fought and bickered the whole time they'd been married, and yet they'd probably had the most amicable and uncomplicated divorce in history.

He headed for the kitchen, set the bag on the kitchen table, pulled out his container of coffee and poured it into a flowered mug. He'd taken his more "manly" mugs with him when he'd left. As he took a sip of coffee, he eyed the dirty dishes sitting in the sink from the day before. In the old days, he would have done them rather than let them sit there. He liked things tidy. Lucy did, too—as long as she didn't have to do the tidying. She had a cleaning service come in twice a week, even though Mike had pointed out that the company she'd chosen overcharged and also overlooked most of the dust and grime in the apartment. Lucy had insisted they were the best in town and that he was too picky.

Mike started out of the kitchen, then turned back, set down his coffee cup, rolled up his sleeves, and marched over to the sink. Old habits died hard.

LUCY WAS BRUSHING HER hair when she heard the water running in the kitchen. She knew Mike was doing the dishes. When she stepped out of the bathroom, she saw her red dress neatly hung on a hanger on the hall tree. She didn't see her panties, but guessed that Mike had put them somewhere. His fanatic neatness used to drive her crazy. She was also feeling a little peeved that he'd sprung out of bed at the ungodly hour of nine in the morning. Couldn't he break his routine even once in his life? They could have had another terrific "dream" together.

Maybe it was just as well they hadn't. She found herself likening sex to potato chips. Once you started, you couldn't stop until . . .

CLARA AND EUNICE WERE standing by the railing on the terrace of their apartment.

"I don't hear a thing," Eunice said, her tone laced with worry.

"They always ate breakfast out on their terrace on Saturdays in nice weather," Clara reminded suspiciously.

"It's still early. Lucy was never an early riser," Eunice commented, biting her lower lip anxiously. She shouldn't be talking about the poor girl in the past tense.

"Wait. I hear someone up there," Clara whispered.

"I DID NOT CALL YOU A slob," Mike said in a tightly controlled voice as he stepped out onto the terrace carrying his coffee and the plate of croissants. Lucy, coffee container in hand, was right at his heels.

"I just suggested," he went on, "that if you didn't want to have to call in an exterminator, you might want to rinse your dishes off right away rather than—"

"I don't see where it's any of your concern," Lucy snapped. "If I feel like piling my dirty dishes in the sink for a week, a month, a year, it's no business of yours."

"You're right. You're right. Anyway, it wouldn't be too big a pile since you only eat in maybe once a week."

Lucy had that all-too-familiar glint in her emerald-green eyes. "Now that you're gone, you can make that once a month."

"Well, the restaurants around town must love you," Mike said dryly. "I know how you like to give big tips. We used to have enough fights over that when I was picking up the tab. If that dress you wore last night is an example, then it's probably safe to assume you're as free with your own money as you were with mine."

"Oh, so now you have some complaints about that dress?"

"My wallet sure would have had some complaints if I'd footed the bill. What did it cost, Lucy? Just for curiosity's sake."

"It's none of your damn business, Mike Powell. You may still handle my business accounts. How I choose to spend money outside of work is no concern of yours."

"Fine. Throw your money away on fancy restaurants, designer clothes—"

"If I recall, you didn't have too many complaints about that dress last night. And another thing," she added, her tone challenging. "Who says *I* leave the tips at restaurants? If you think I've been dining solo since our divorce, you're sadly mistaken."

"Oh, believe me, Lucy," Mike steamed, "I'm not sad. I'm ecstatic. I'm thrilled you've found some sucker to take my place. I'm— Lucy, put that plate down. I'm warning you, Lucy. You've thrown your very last piece of china at me. You let go of that plate or I warn you, you'll be sorry."

EUNICE CLUTCHED CLARA'S sleeve as they heard first a crash overhead and then a loud feminine shriek. "Oh, dear. Oh, no. What should we do?"

"Hurry, call the police," Clara ordered, nudging her companion into the apartment.

"I DON'T BELIEVE IT," Lucy said indignantly.

"I did warn you," Mike said self-righteously.

"I haven't been . . . spanked since I was ten years old."

He leaned closer to her, nose to nose. "Well, if you ask me, it's been too long. Besides," he added, "you had it coming. You threw that plate at me."

"I only wish I'd had better aim."

They stared at each other, both of them fuming.

"I don't know who was in that bed with me last night," Lucy muttered acerbically. "It wasn't the normal you. I guess it was the champagne."

"That's a nice thing to say, Lucy. So, what are you really telling me? That while we were married I was a lousy lover?"

"I wouldn't say lousy. Just . . . conservative." Lucy cursed silently. Why had she said that? It wasn't even true. Mike had been a good lover, even if last night he'd risen to new heights. She knew why she'd said it, though. She was mad. And when she got mad she struck out. Plates, words . . .

"I guess it was the champagne," Mike said tightly. "I must have been drunk to have come back here with you last night. I'm real sober now. Sober enough to see that nothing's one drop different. You'll never change."

"Neither will you. You vary about as much as the vernal equinox."

"Because I'm steady, reliable, responsible. I take that as a compliment, Lucy."

"You would."

"Just think, Lucy. If we hadn't wised up and gotten this divorce, we might have spent another thirty, forty years together making each other miserable." Even as he spat out those words, he couldn't help also thinking about what it might have been like spending the next thirty to forty years making wild, passionate love together as they had last night. He cursed himself for getting aroused even as his rage mounted.

They continued their face-off in silence for a few more minutes, Mike digging his hands in his pockets, Lucy holding her arms folded across her chest.

"I think you'd better leave, Mr. Powell, before I say something I might be sorry for," she said finally.

The very nerve of her, Mike thought. So, she wasn't even the least bit sorry for any of the crummy things she'd said so far.

"You bet I'll go," he replied hoarsely. "And wild horses won't get me back here."

"That's fine with me."

Mike slammed the front door on his way out, missing the sneaker Lucy had kicked off her foot and was flinging in his direction. As he rode down the elevator, Mike's fury quickly turned to melancholy. He tried to figure out how both he and Lucy had managed to take a perfectly splendid night and transform it into a perfect horror of a morning. Maybe if he hadn't done those damn dishes. That seemed to have been what set her off. Something else probably would have come up, he conceded. He'd felt tense from the moment he'd gotten out of bed. And Lucy had certainly seemed tense. The way she'd marched into the kitchen, you'd think he'd committed a crime instead of washed off a few dishes.

Had they each been itching for a fight? Had last night, as incredible as it had been, scared the living daylights out of both of them? If they hadn't fought this morning, what would have happened? Something, apparently, neither of them was ready for, Mike concluded.

As he stepped out of the elevator into the lobby he was dismayed to find himself face-to-face with The Odd Couple once again. Eunice Blanford and Clara Ponds practically accosted him as he started across the lobby.

"Are you leaving again?" Eunice asked, her voice warbly.

"Well, I . . . Yes. Yes, I am leaving, ladies. This time, for good," Mike said somberly.

Eunice shot Clara an anxious glance. Clara paled.

"Well, that's . . . a pity," Clara muttered. "Because . . . because Eunice and I were hoping you'd—"

"Have tea with us. Yes, a nice, settling cup of tea." Eunice said, unable to come up with another idea to delay him.

"Yes," Clara said, clearing her throat. "Tea."

"I made these lovely little scones," Eunice babbled. "With currants. Some people substitute raisins for currants, but they're not the same thing at all."

"No, not at all," Clara agreed.

"Scones without currents, my Oliver always used to say, may he rest in peace— Oh dear," Eunice muttered, pressing her lips together. *Bringing up the dearly departed at a time like this.*

"That's very nice of you, Mrs. Ponds," Mike said politely, "but . . ." The rest of his sentence was drowned out by the sound of sirens outside the building. The next thing he knew, the two old ladies had each taken a surprisingly firm hold of his arms as two uniformed police officers burst through the front door, rushing past the startled doorman, their guns at the ready.

A robbery, Mike supposed, thinking the two women were gripping him so tightly because they were alarmed by the sudden appearance of the cops.

"It's okay, ladies," he started to reassure them, only to find the two officers heading straight for them.

"Hands up!" the younger of the two policemen barked.

Mike was stunned. What had The Odd Couple gone and done? It was only when the two women released him, stepping quickly out of the way and he saw that the two officers were pointing their guns directly at him and not the old ladies, that Mike realized he was the one being issued the order.

Dazed, he swallowed hard, doing as they demanded, since there really wasn't much else he could do. "What's this about? What did I do?" Obviously, they had him confused with someone else. Surely, Clara Ponds and Eunice Blanford would vouch for him.

"We thought you'd never get here," Clara scolded the men in blue.

"Yes, you were almost too late," Eunice said, then pressed her free hand to her mouth. "Oh dear, you may still be *too late!*"

Mike stared at the two women with utter bewilderment. This quickly gave way to terror when the older officer spun him around and nudged him not so gently up against the wall beside the elevator.

"Okay, hands flat against the wall and spread 'em."

"Look, this must be some crazy mistake," Mike said as the younger officer started to frisk him. "I didn't do anything. I've never even gotten a parking ticket. I don't even own a car." There was an edge of panic in his voice. "You can at least tell me what you think I've done."

"We thought they were such a nice couple," Eunice murmured earnestly.

"I thought no such thing," Clara said. "They were always fighting and throwing things. And then she threw him out."

"Lucy? She didn't throw me out," Mike protested. "We both agreed to a divorce and I left. Since when is divorce a crime?"

The officer frisking him removed something from Mike's pants pocket that caused the two old women to gasp in unison. Mike glanced over his shoulder to see what it was. He turned red. Almost as red as Lucy's red silk panties, which the officer was holding in his hand.

"Okay buddy," the cop said. "You want to explain these?"

"GO ON AND LAUGH. I want you to know I find nothing amusing about it," Mike snapped at his chuckling uncle. "And I sure as hell wasn't laughing when two of New York's Finest dragged me up to Lucy's apartment, those two old biddies following along, to see if I had gone and murdered my ex-wife—and taken her undies along as a souvenir of the kill. I have never been so scared, so humiliated, so furious—"

"Mikey, Mikey. One of these days you'll be laughing about it, too."

Mike maintained a grim expression as he wagged a finger at his uncle. "This whole thing was your fault. Teaneck, New Jersey. If you hadn't set us up last night, none of this would have happened."

"Whoa. You did have a hand in it, Mikey," Uncle Paulie countered. "I just arranged for you and Lucy to have a couple of hours together here at the club. To talk things over. See where each of you was at. I didn't arrange for the two of you to head over to Lucy's apartment after you closed up shop."

"No, but you were hoping...."

"Without hope, Mikey, we'd be lost. And pretty darn miserable. Hope should always spring eternal, kid."

Mike propped his elbows on the bar and dropped his head into the palms of his hands. "I don't even know why we were fighting. I don't understand it."

Then Mike sighed. "Oh, I understand it. I just wish she wasn't ... Or that I wasn't ..."

He lifted his head and eyed his smiling uncle. "Okay, okay, so I'm still crazy about her."

"I never doubted it for an instant. Any more than I doubted that she's still crazy about you."

"It's not enough, Uncle Paulie." He toyed with the cocktail napkin that had accompanied his glass of ginger ale. "Maybe I *am* too picky, too rigid, too tight, too... conservative."

"It probably wouldn't cause the stock market to collapse if you loosened up a bit," Paulie said with an affectionate smile.

Mike rubbed his jaw. "I'll tell you something, Uncle Paulie. Last night ... Well, last night ..." He smiled sheepishly.

"You trying to tell me that last night was magic, Mikey? That maybe for once in your life you jumped out of the plane without your parachute and you didn't come crashing down to the ground?"

"Not last night, anyway," Mike admitted. "I sure crashed this morning, though."

Uncle Paulie ruffled his nephew's hair. "That's because you put your parachute back on, kid. You got so uptight you didn't bother to notice that you were within safe landing distance and you didn't need to load yourself up with all your gear. You know what I'm saying? It's like the guy clinging to a ledge, terrified to let go, and he doesn't even know he's only a couple of feet above the ground."

Mike nodded. "That's me, all right."

"Like you said, it wasn't you last night. What that says to me, kid, is that you've got this other hidden side—wild, flamboyant, devil-may-care. And Lucy really went for it, didn't she?" Uncle Paulie added, grinning.

"Yeah, she went for it, all right," Mike mused. "She blamed it on the champagne."

"Answer me one question, Mikey. Answer it straight from the heart. You want her back?"

"It's not that simple, Uncle Paulie."

"Come on, Mikey. A simple yes or no."

Mike's head dropped. His shoulders sagged. It was simple. "Yes, Uncle Paulie. I want her back."

Uncle Paulie grinned, rubbing his hands together. "Okay, okay. So, all we need now is a plan."

"If it involves Teaneck . . ."

STILL CLAD IN HER SHORTS and T-shirt, Lucy rang Stephie's doorbell. As soon as Stephie opened the door and took one look at her soulful friend, she quickly ushered her past the living room where Jerry and Amy were building a Tinkertoy fort. Father and daughter called out a greeting to Lucy, but all she could manage in response was a weak smile and a weaker wave.

Once they got to the kitchen, Stephie swung the door shut and gave her friend a close scrutiny.

"What's wrong?" she demanded in her typical get-right-to-the-point manner.

"Do I look that bad?" Lucy asked, dropping into a chair at the kitchen table, sweeping away the half-empty cereal bowl on the blue plastic place mat in front of her. Stephie hadn't cleaned up from breakfast yet.

"You can never look *that* bad, and don't think I don't hate you for it," Stephie teased. "It's just that I was hoping you'd be glowing this morning," she admitted, pouring them both coffees and then sitting down across from her friend.

"You knew? You knew about Uncle Paulie and that dumb story about Teaneck?" Somehow, Lucy wasn't all that surprised.

"You didn't fall for it?" Stephie frowned. "I told Paulie he needed a better—"

"I did fall for it. So did Mike. That's the problem." Lucy rose from the chair and started pacing. "How could you have been a party to such a stupid, dumb, idiotic plan?" She came to an abrupt stop. "I thought you were my best friend," she said, accusation and hurt in her voice.

"Will you sit down, Lucy. I *am* your best friend. And best friends should be honest with each other."

Lucy dropped back into her chair. "We slept together last night."

Stephie smiled. "That's honest."

"It was great. It was more than great. It was—"

"Okay, okay, you don't have to be that honest. I'm two months pregnant and let's just say my own sex life at the moment isn't at its height. You know, it loses something when you've got to tap your hubby on the shoulder and say, 'Hold that position without me for a minute while I go throw up.'

With Amy I only had morning sickness in the morning. This time it's more like round-the-clock sickness."

Lucy stared at Stephie. "You're going to have another baby? You didn't even tell me."

"I didn't even know for sure until yesterday. I thought it was the flu. Amy and Jerry both had it and when I first started feeling queasy I thought my turn had come. Yesterday, on a whim, I decided I'd just pick up one of those at-home pregnancy tests. Some whim!"

Lucy started to cry.

Stephie jumped up, stepped behind Lucy's chair and put her arms around her friend. "Hey, it's okay. I want this baby."

Lucy kept crying. "I do, too."

"You want my baby?"

"No. I want a baby of my own."

"They're easy enough to make," Stephie quipped.

"I want a baby with Mike."

"That makes it even easier."

"It isn't easy at all," Lucy wailed. "He hates everything about me. Well, maybe not everything." She plucked a napkin from the yellow plastic napkin holder in the center of the table and dabbed at her eyes. "I don't know, Steph. Maybe it is my fault. I can be too hotheaded at times, too extravagant, too self-indulgent, too. . . ." She cast her friend a rueful look. "Stop me when you think I've gone too far."

Stephie grinned. "I thought you were just getting warmed up."

Lucy sighed. "If only I had this morning to do all over again. We got into such a stupid argument. And I started it. All the poor guy was doing was the dumb dishes. And then there was all that crazy business with The Odd Couple, the police and my panties. What a morning. What an absolutely insane morning! Mike was livid when he left."

"Whoa," Stephie said. "Back up a little. The Odd Couple, the police and your panties?"

Lucy grinned, despite her misery. "The old biddies in the apartment below us thought Mike had done me in."

"What in heaven's name made them think that?"

"Circumstantial evidence, mostly. They heard a crash and then they heard me scream. I only screamed because Mike had the nerve to spank me. Well, it wasn't really much of a spank. Of course, I did throw a plate of croissants at him. I missed hitting him, though. I always miss him. I've got lousy aim. And he's got great reflexes. That's why I do it—throw things. If I really thought I could hit him, I wouldn't. Anyway, they thought he'd murdered me in a fit of jealous rage. The Odd Couple, that is. Eunice and Clara. And then when the police found my red panties stuffed in Mike's trouser pocket . . ."

"Should I ask why your red panties were in his pocket or is it too kinky for my delicate ears?"

Lucy sighed. "I never did find out what they were doing there. And now I'll never know. Our parting words were pretty...final. And pretty dramatic," Lucy added, "with two irritated policemen and my trouble-making neighbors looking on. Not that The Odd Couple didn't have my interests and safety at heart. And they did fall all over themselves apologizing to us both, once they saw that I was alive and kicking. Just imagine Mike, who wouldn't hurt a fly, as a murderer! It really was pretty funny. Only no one was laughing." And Lucy didn't feel anywhere close to laughing now.

Stephie gave her shoulder a little shake. "Oh, come on, Luce. You two slept together last night. You said it was great. Better than great. So you had a little spat this morning. Maybe things got out of hand. At least this time, you see that you do bear some of the responsibility for the clashes you two keep having. There's nothing to say you can't change—if you want to."

Lucy was doubtful. "Even if I could change, Mike isn't likely to believe it. I've made such a big deal about telling him how he was the one that needed to change, not me. Even if I were willing . . . Even if I could . . . How am I going to prove to him that I can be more . . . less . . . ? Well, you know what I mean."

"Simple," Stephie said. "Seeing is believing."

"Seeing is the problem. We both vowed we'd never have anything more to do with each other as long as we lived."

Stephie coiled a strand of hair around her index finger. "Okay, so it isn't going to be simple. Hell, Luce. You've always been a gal who loved a challenge. My money's on you. You'll think of something." She uncoiled the strand of hair from her finger. "Of course, we could always confer with Uncle Paulie. He might have a couple more ideas up his sleeve."

"Oh, no. Uncle Paulie had his chance at playing Cupid." Lucy rose from the table, a determined expression on her face. "I got myself in this fix. And I'll figure a way out of it."

6

ABOUT A WEEK LATER Lucy figured a possible way out of her dilemma. It was pretty wild, utterly farfetched, and it probably wouldn't work, but she was desperate. A desperate woman in love. She got the idea from a layout she was going over for a soft-drink magazine advertisement featuring Daphne Cole, one of her top models.

After studying the layout for a good twenty minutes, Lucy started scribbling notes on a piece of paper. She studied her notes, then grabbed up her purse and took the rest of the afternoon off. She had a lot to do.

By the next day Lucy was ready to put her plan into action. She wasn't ready to try it out on Mike until she felt more confident of pulling it off. She decided to use Stephie for her acid test.

She dialed her friend's number. Stephie answered on the second ring. "How would you like to be treated to lunch at Chez Pauline's this afternoon?" Lucy asked brightly.

"If Mel Gibson's treating, the answer is yes. Even if he changes his mind and wants to go Dutch, the answer is yes."

"Sorry. According to *People*, Mel's at home on his range in Australia taking a break between films. Will you settle for getting treated by your closest and dearest friend?"

"Luce. I thought you were turning over a new leaf. What you'd blow on a lunch at Chez Pauline's I could feed my family of three and a half on for a week."

Lucy grinned. "Speaking of the half, how's she doing?"

"This week it's a he. Actually, I haven't thrown up in three days. And a gourmet lunch at Chez Pauline's actually does sound tempting...."

"Please say yes, Steph. I've got a surprise for you."

"What surprise?" Stephie asked cautiously. "You sound funny, Luce."

Lucy gave herself a critical appraisal in her mirror and smiled. She looked kind of funny, too. "If I tell you what the surprise is, silly, it won't be a surprise."

Stephie balked. "I hate surprises. Surprises make me very uncomfortable. I never say or do the right things. Remember that surprise party you threw me for my twenty-fifth. I turned all red and I almost—"

"One o'clock sharp. Don't be late."

Stephie laughed. "You're telling *me* not to be late? Lucy, you were late for your wedding."

"I know, Steph. I'm turning over a new leaf."

AT FIVE MINUTES AFTER ONE that afternoon, Stephie stepped into the posh Chez Pauline, one of midtown Manhattan's trendiest and most expensive new dining spots. The restaurant was done in a stylish French deco, with curved gray leather banquettes providing cosy nooks against pale pink walls. The design on the carpeting featured interlocking geometric pink diamonds on a charcoal-gray background. As the slender, refined, silver-haired maître d' approached, Stephie was already surveying the dining room. She wasn't surprised not to see Lucy among the diners. To Lucy, being on time meant give or take an hour.

"May I help you?"

"I'm meeting Miss Warner. I believe she made a reservation for one o'clock."

The maître d' quickly scanned his guest list. "Ah, yes, Miss Ellen Warner. She arrived about ten minutes ago. She's waiting at your table. This way, please."

Stephie tugged his sleeve, the only way she could get his attention, as he had already done a graceful pirouette and was starting to lead her off to the wrong table.

"I'm sorry, but you've got the wrong Warner. I'm meeting a Miss Lucy Warner."

The maître d's brows knitted together as he once again scanned his reservation book. "I don't have a Miss Lucy Warner . . ."

"Oh, maybe she booked it under the name Powell," Stephie suggested. "Lucy Powell."

The maître d' did a third check, his irritation beginning to show. "We have no reservations for a Miss Lucy Powell. Perhaps it is her first name you have confused. Shall I show you to Miss Ellen Warner's table or would you prefer—"

Stephie waved him on impatiently, thinking it was the maître d' who could have gotten the first names mixed up. Not that he looked the type to make mistakes, but then looks could be deceiving!

As Stephie approached Ellen Warner's table, she saw a young woman with light brown hair pulled back severely from her face. Her gray-green eyes were hidden behind librarian-style horn-rimmed glasses and she was encased in a prim, gray, conservative business suit over a white silk blouse. Stephie was about to apologize for the mistake when Ellen Warner looked up and smiled at her.

There was something awfully familiar about that smile. . . .

"You must be Stephie Benson."

Stephie was thrown by the clipped British accent. "Yes . . ."

"Please, sit down. Lucy should be here any minute."

Stephie hesitated, then slid into the banquette, a sly expression on her face. "Come on. Is this some kind of a gag, Luce?"

"Do we still look that much alike, then?"

Stephie laughed, certain Lucy was pulling her leg. "Well, I hope I won't be hurting your feelings if I tell you that Lucy's got a lot more pizzazz. Really, dear, that outfit and hairstyle don't do anything for you. And those glasses. If I were you, I'd ditch them as fast as I could. They make you look like an owl. And not one of your prettier owls."

"Oh . . ." Tears welled up in Ellen Warner's eyes. "I suppose, being Lucy's twin...you expected we'd... I...I never did have Lucy's . . . panache. I guess . . . she still has it."

Stephie felt a sinking in the pit of her stomach. "If this is some kind of gag, Lucy Warner, I am never going to forgive you."

"She never told you about me, did she?" Ellen sighed. "Oh, I'm not surprised. We had this bloody falling-out when we were seventeen and . . . Well, Lucy could be very hotheaded in those days...and impulsive. It's ironic being twins and yet being so . . . different. Lucy and I haven't spoken in over ten years. Since I'm in town on business—I'm legal counsel to the McGurtry Foundation—I thought it was time Lucy and I had a rapprochement. I phoned her and she was rather taken aback. But she did say she was meeting her good friend Stephie Benson for lunch at Chez Pauline's, and if I liked I could join you both." Ellen leaned a bit closer to Stephie. "My guess is she thought you would serve as a buffer. Last time we were alone together things got . . . out of hand. Lucy threw one of Mother's best china pitchers at me. Oh, she missed. She had lousy aim. But she did hit one of Mother's favorite Limoges vases. Mother was fit to be tied."

Stephie didn't know what to say. Still dubious, she had to admit this "twin" was mighty convincing. "So, where is she? Lucy?"

Ellen sighed. "I suppose you know Lucy better than I do at this point, but I do remember that she never was terribly prompt. Do you know, she was late for her high school graduation?"

"And her wedding," Stephie added. "Something tells me you already knew that."

Ellen smiled wistfully. "No. No, I didn't. But I'm not surprised."

"Okay, okay. Hold on. You want me to believe you're Lucy's twin sister from London and that the two of you had such a terrible falling-out that she didn't even invite you to her wedding, never breathed so much as a word about your existence to me, her very best friend—"

"She did tell my mother I could come to her wedding if I wanted to, but she didn't even have the courtesy to send me an invitation. I'm sure you can understand that I couldn't attend."

Stephie scratched her head. "I can't understand anything."

A waitress approached. Ellen checked her watch. "I suppose we might as well see what we want to order." She asked the waitress to give them a couple of minutes to decide.

Stephie eyed the menu, mainly the prices next to each of the items. If this wasn't the gag of the century and the woman beside her really was Lucy's twin sister, she was a little edgy about who was going to foot the bill if the real Lucy didn't show up. With a second baby on the way, she'd promised Jerry she would stick to their budget. Which didn't include fancy dinners at chichi restaurants.

"Lucy certainly has expensive tastes," Ellen muttered. "Good thing I can charge our meal to my expense account."

Stephie smiled. "Right. Good thing."

They were through the soup course when Ellen turned to Stephie. "Do you think she isn't coming at all?"

Stephie smiled ruefully. "Gee, it sure looks that way."

"She probably got cold feet. Lucy never was one to forgive easily."

"Neither are her friends," Stephie said dryly. At this point, she was again convinced Lucy was trying to pull the wool over her eyes.

"I think I'll ring her up."

Stephie shrugged. "Go on. But something tells me she won't be home."

A minute later, a mournful-looking Ellen returned to the table.

"Not home?" Stephie queried airily, digging into her chicken Marsala.

"That's the problem. She *is* at home."

"Really," Stephie said, slipping a piece of the chicken into her mouth.

"Yes. She's refusing to come. Says she just isn't ready to . . . to have an awkward encounter with me. She says she doesn't want to risk a scene."

Stephie nodded, chewing and smiling. She had to hand it to Lucy. She was doing her best to pull off this charade. The phone call was a nice touch.

"The thing is . . . Would you speak with her, Stephie? I asked her to hold on."

Stephie nearly choked on the piece of chicken she was swallowing. "She . . . Lucy . . . is waiting on the phone?"

Ellen nodded. "Please, Stephie. Maybe you can convince her I'm not going to cause a scene. Honestly, do I look like the kind of person who would want to bring unwanted attention to myself?"

Stephie narrowed her gaze on Ellen. "Okay, here's the deal. If Lucy Warner is not on the other end of the line, that's the end of it. Do I make myself perfectly clear, Ellen?"

"Oh, yes. Perfectly clear, Stephie."

"Fine." Stephie rose from the table and headed across the dining room to the pair of phone booths. Ellen followed her, pointing to the booth where Lucy was supposedly on the other end of the line.

Before Stephie stepped into the booth, Ellen gripped her arm. "I do love Lucy, Stephie. And I know you do, too."

Stephie stepped into the booth, closed the door, and picked up the receiver that was resting on the metal shelf beneath the phone. She felt pretty silly saying, "Hello, Luce? Are you there?"

No response. Not that Stephie was surprised.

Stephie was just about to hang up and give the real Lucy a piece of her mind when she heard a voice asking, "Steph. Is that you?"

Stephie almost dropped the phone. "Lucy? Lucy, where the hell are you?"

"I'm here. At home. What do you think of my...surprise? You know. My sister, Ellen?"

Stephie paled. "She . . . really is your sister?"

"We've been...estranged for years. I just can't face her yet, Steph. What...what is she like now? She used to be so...stiff and proper. Just like my father."

"Oh, Lucy, I don't believe this. I thought it was you. I was so sure— Oh, no, Luce. I just said some of the most awful things to her, thinking you were pulling my leg. I insulted her horribly—her appearance, her clothes, her glasses. I called her an owl. I called her an ugly owl."

"Oh, Steph, does she really look that awful?"

Stephie sighed. "No, not really. She does look a lot like you, actually."

"We *are* twins."

"It's just that she's so laid-back, so sensible looking, so conservative. She looks like a lawyer."

"She *is* a lawyer. Ellen never did condone my going in for modeling instead of 'using my brains,' as she put it."

"She does seem very... smart," Stephie confessed. "And together."

"Kind of like that woman Mike was with at Penny Laine's party a few months back?"

"Now that you mention it, yes."

"Maybe Mike married the wrong twin," Lucy murmured.

"Oh, come on, Luce."

"She is more his type. Smart, sensible, goal oriented, and I'm sure she's still as frugal as ever. Admit it, Stephie. They would be a good match."

"Lucy—"

"No, really, Steph. You won't hurt my feelings. Don't you agree that if Mike met Ellen he'd be... drawn to her?"

"Oh, Luce, don't ask me things like that."

"You've always been straight with me, Steph."

"Okay, maybe she's more Mike's type. Maybe too much his type. My bet is he'd be bored by Ellen after a couple of hours. He isn't seeing that gal he brought to Penny's party anymore, is he?"

"No, but I'm sure he's seeing other Royces, though."

"Look, forget about Mike for a minute. What about your sister? She really wants to see you, Luce. If you grab a cab, you could make it here for dessert."

"Do you like her, Steph?"

"Yes, I like her. She's your twin sister."

"Did you really think I was pulling one over on you, Steph?"

"Of course, I did. I never would have insulted her like that otherwise. I feel just awful. Come on, Lucy. Grab that cab and come down here. My very expensive and very tasty chicken Marsala is getting cold."

"Go on back. Tell Ellen I'll . . . try to make it."

"Okay, but try hard."

"I'll try my best."

Stephie hung up and stepped out of the phone booth. Ellen came hurrying over to her. "So? Is she coming?"

"She'll try to make it for dessert."

Ellen smiled and grabbed Stephie's hand. "I knew you'd talk her into it. The two of you must really be special friends."

They went back to their table, chatting amiably while they finished their lunches. The waitress came over to clear their table and take their dessert order. Stephie checked her watch and frowned.

"We won't wait for her," Ellen said, ordering lemon meringue pie.

Stephie observed Ellen curiously.

"What is it?" Ellen asked.

"Nothing. It's just that it's Lucy's favorite dessert."

"Yes. I know." She turned her attention back to the waitress. "And a crème brulé for my friend."

Stephie's mouth opened. "That's my . . . favorite dessert."

Ellen smiled. "Yes. I know." Slowly, she removed her owlish glasses and then slipped the combs out of her chignon, letting her hair tumble down to her shoulders. "Presto chango," Ellen said. Sans the British accent. "I thought the brown hair rinse was a nice touch. And the colored contact lenses."

Stephie just stared at her.

"I really did pull it off, didn't I? You bought it, Steph." Lucy giggled. "You should see your face."

Stephie was still trying to take it all in. "But . . . but the phone call?"

"I did think that was brilliant," Lucy said proudly. "I just dialed the phone booth next to yours and stepped in there when you picked up the phone in the booth beside me."

"I don't believe this," Stephie muttered.

"Do I really look like an owl in these glasses?" Lucy asked, removing them and scrutinizing the frames. "Maybe I should switch to gold rims. Or clear plastic."

The waitress brought their desserts over.

Stephie stared at her crème brulé. "If this didn't look totally divine, I'd drop this custard right on top of your phony brown-rinsed hair, Lucy Warner. That was the cheapest, lowest, crummiest—"

"I gather you're bloody mad at me," Lucy teased in her British accent.

"I should be." She eyed Lucy questioningly. "There really *is* no twin, even in London?"

"No twin." Lucy took a bite of her lemon meringue pie. "Mmm. Delicious."

Stephie watched her friend chew. "Just tell me why, Lucy? Is this 'Make Stephie Benson Feel Like An Idiot' Day?"

"No, Steph. This is 'Make Mike Powell Fall In Love With Ellen' Day."

Stephie blinked rapidly several times. "You're not serious, Lucy."

"Ellen is everything I'm not, Steph. More important, she's everything Mike wishes I'd be."

"This is crazy. You know this is crazy."

"Why? Don't you think that if I can convince my very closest friend in the world that I'm Ellen Warner—Lucy's levelheaded, practical, serious-minded, frugal twin—that I can convince my ex-husband? I know he doesn't look the type, but I have known Mike to be gullible. Whereas you're the last person I would call gullible, Steph, and look at how brilliantly..."

Stephie swallowed a spoonful of her crème brulé. "Okay, okay. Don't rub it in. I want you to know that I had very serious reservations—"

"Only at first. Admit it, I had you eating out of Ellen's hand by the time we got to our main course."

"Please. I eat off plates not people's hands."

Lucy grinned. "I think I can pull it off with Mike. I was a little nervous about it until now."

"Okay, let's say you pull it off. Let's say Mike is actually gullible enough to believe you've got this stuffy twin sister—"

"Ellen isn't stuffy, Stephie," Lucy quipped. "She's really a terrific woman, once you get to know her. Or I should say, once Mike gets to know her. She's simplicity personified. She thinks before she leaps. She doesn't go flying off the handle. She doesn't throw china."

"You've set yourself a tall order, Luce. What makes you think you can be all those things you aren't?"

"I love him, Steph. I love him enough to be all those things. I want him back," Lucy said earnestly. "You said yourself I'd come up with a way."

And when he finds out there really is no Ellen?" Stephie queried gently.

"By then I'll have convinced him that I—Lucy Warner—really can be the kind of woman he wants me to be. We'll get married again and live happily ever after."

"A nice fairy tale, kiddo. In real life, fairy tales are at a premium, you know."

"I'm bound and determined to make my fairy tale come true, Steph. Will you help me?"

"Help you how?" Stephie asked warily.

MIKE SLIPPED HIS SUIT jacket back on as he rose from behind his desk. A moment later the door to his office opened.

"Stephie, what a surprise!" He stepped around the desk to greet Lucy's friend.

"Hi, Mike. How are you doing?" Stephie asked brightly.

A little too brightly, Mike thought.

"Oh . . . Okay, I guess." His complexion got a little ruddy. "I suppose you heard about my run-in with the law last Saturday morning."

Stephie pretended not to understand. "Your what?"

"Come on, Stephie. Lucy had to have told you. She tells you everything."

"Lucy's flown the coop. Which is why I'm here." Stephie produced a dramatic sigh.

"Flown the . . . ?" Mike gestured to a chair across from his desk. "Please, sit down, Stephie."

She took him up on his offer and Mike followed suit, returning to the chair behind his desk. His expression was a mix of worry and confusion as he asked, "Where is she, Stephie? What do you mean, 'She's flown the coop'?"

"Oh, don't worry. It's temporary. She dropped me a note saying that she'd be back in a few days."

"Where is she?"

"She didn't say. My guess is she's staying at that artist friend's place out in the Hamptons."

"Jack Nealon's cottage?"

Stephie nodded. "Like I said, that's my guess."

"Is she...with Jack?" Mike could feel all his muscles tense. Jack Nealon and Lucy had been friends for years. Had they become more than friends? Had she turned to Jack on the rebound after their catastrophic get-together last weekend?

"No," Stephie replied, her tone reassuring. "I read in the paper that Jack's out in San Francisco for a one-man show. From the note Lucy sent me, it sounded more like she just needed some time to herself. Reading between the lines, she seemed a bit . . . agitated. At first I thought it was because of the two of you getting together last week."

"So, you did know that much."

Stephie smiled sheepishly. "Paulie kind of discussed it with me before he set it up."

Mike frowned.

"We both thought he was doing the right thing," Stephie said contritely. "But I guess we shouldn't have meddled." If that was meddling, what would Mike call this? She shuddered to think!

"You guessed right. You shouldn't have meddled," Mike said, his voice lacking conviction. "Our get-together was a disaster." He shrugged. "Anyway, that's beside the point. You said before, you were here because Lucy flew the coop. I don't understand—"

"I was coming to that," Stephie interrupted. "You see, when I first got that note from Lucy, I thought she was just . . . well, getting a little distance from you. So that she could think things through. Then I discovered you weren't the only one she was trying to distance herself from."

"You're losing me, Stephie."

"It's just that I don't know what to do about it, Mike. About *her*, I mean."

"Her? Lucy?"

"No, not Lucy. Ellen. I don't know what to do about Ellen. I thought maybe you—"

"Ellen who?"

"Ellen, Lucy's twin sister. That's who," Stephie said impatiently.

"What? Who?"

"Please, Mike, don't tell me Lucy kept Ellen a secret from you."

Mike rose from his chair. "Hold on, Stephie. Somebody's pulling your leg. Lucy doesn't have a twin sister. She doesn't have any sisters. Or brothers. Lucy's an only child."

Stephie manufactured a shocked expression. "I can't believe this."

"It's true. Believe me," Mike said with a smile.

"No, I can't believe Lucy never told you about Ellen."

"Stephie."

"Mike, sit down," Stephie said in the firm voice she used with her two-year-old when she was going to give her a serious lecture on such vagaries as sticking one's fingers in electrical outlets.

Mike hesitated, then sat down. Stephie, wondering how she ever let Lucy talk her into this insanity, edged her seat closer to Mike's desk and proceeded to enlighten him about the wholly unexpected arrival from London, England, of Lucy's "prodigal" twin sister, Ellen.

7

"MIKEY, GET REAL," Uncle Paulie said with a chuckle from behind the bar. Tonight he was dressed Western-style right down to the fringed shirt and the rawhide tie. A jazz group with a country-and-western flavor was appearing this evening.

"I'm just telling you—"

"Stephie's pulling your leg, kid. I refuse to believe Lucy would have kept a twin sister a secret from you. It doesn't make sense."

Mike shrugged. "Lucy and I never did talk all that much about our pasts. And she never actually told me she was an only child. I took it for granted. Like she took it for granted I don't have any siblings."

"And you don't," Paulie pointed out.

"But I could. I could have a brother or sister out there somewhere that for whatever reason, I chose to ignore. According to Stephie, Lucy and her sister had a falling-out when they were seventeen and haven't spoken to each other since."

"That part is possible. But Lucy not telling you—"

"Stephie says Lucy would have eventually gotten around to it, but she and Ellen always had this love-hate relationship and she felt—Lucy, that is—that since Ellen wouldn't even accept her invitation to our wedding—"

"Her own twin sister wouldn't come to her wedding?" Paulie leaned his elbows on the marble bar and peered at his nephew who sat across from him, perched on a barstool.

"According to Stephie… Well, actually according to what Ellen told Stephie," Mike said, "she didn't come to the wedding because Lucy didn't invite her personally. She sent an offhanded note to her mother saying if Ellen wanted to come along, she could. Ellen felt that if Lucy really wanted a rapprochement, she would have invited her in a more direct, straightforward manner."

Paulie studied Mike with incredulity. "You don't seriously buy any of this, do you?"

Mike sighed. "I don't know. Why would Stephie make it up?"

"I tell you, Lucy's got something up her sleeve," Paulie insisted. "And Stephie's playing straight man."

"Well, I guess we'll know for sure pretty soon. She's meeting me here in—" Mike checked his watch "—ten minutes. Ellen, that is."

Promptly at seven-fifteen, "Ellen" Warner stepped inside the Bennett Street Club & Grill. The place didn't fill up until after eight so Mike had no trouble spotting her from where he was sitting at the bar.

"Uncle Paulie," he hissed. "Look. Over by the entrance."

Paulie put down the cloth he was using to dust off the liquor bottles and had a gander at the woman who was standing just inside the door, nervously glancing around the club. Their eyes met. He grinned, motioning her over. At the same time, he muttered under his breath to his nephew, "She looks like Lucy might look on an off day. If Lucy ever *had* an off day."

As she approached, Mike rose so abruptly his elbow knocked over his cola. The brown liquid spilled down over the edge of the bar onto his khaki trousers, leaving an altogether-embarrassing stain in his lap.

"Oh, dear. What a bloody shame," Lucy said, her clipped British accent even heavier than the one she'd used on

Stephie. Lucy was afraid Mike would be a harder sell. As close as she and Stephie were, she and Mike had lived together, sharing every intimacy for almost a year.

Mike, usually so meticulous, gave his stained trousers the briefest of glances, his gaze fixing on the woman who was supposedly Lucy's twin sister. She was just as Stephie had described her. The same height and build, but the hair was a shade or two darker, the eyes more gray than green behind gold-rimmed glasses. Uncle Paulie was right. She looked like Lucy on an off day. And he was right again, when he said that Lucy never had an off day. Certainly not as off as this. Still, he regarded her with unmasked suspicion. Lucy had pulled some pretty sneaky pranks in the past. Was this little disguise her way of taking the edge off their awful fight last week? Did this mean she wanted to kiss and make up? Or did she blame him for that embarrassing "panty" episode, and want to get back at him? Or was this payback for all those times he'd told her that she should make a few changes?

He stared at her for so long without saying anything that Uncle Paulie filled in the silence, stretching his hand across the bar and extending it to Lucy. "I'm Lucy's ex-uncle-in-law, Paulie. This guy covered in cola is Lucy's ex-husband, Mike." A slight pause. "In case you didn't know," he added with a sardonic smile.

Lucy took Paulie's hand, giving it an extra-firm Ellen-style shake. "A pleasure to meet you, Paulie." She gave Mike a hesitant smile. It was one she'd worked on all afternoon in front of a mirror after Stephie had told her that her real smile was too much of a giveaway. This was as un-Lucy a smile as she could master.

"Nice to meet you, too, Mike." She extended her hand to his. "Stephie did describe you, but she . . . didn't do you justice."

Mike stared at her outstretched hand for a moment before it registered that she wanted to shake his hand. As they shook hands, her gaze dropped to his slacks. "You really ought to go wash that stain off before it sets, Mike. Pity to ruin a perfectly lovely and no-doubt-expensive pair of trousers." A nice touch, Lucy thought. A chance to show that she was not the wastrel her sister was. As Lucy, she might have told him to just chuck the pants and buy himself a new pair. Funny, but dressed as Ellen, using the British accent, playing the role of a twin sister so opposite in personality from her real self, Lucy really did feel like she was becoming this invented persona. There always had been more than a little ham in her. Method acting, some would call it. Not Mike, though. She didn't want to think what he would call it—at least, not until she'd won him over.

Mike had difficulty tearing his eyes away from Lucy, but when he did look down at his slacks, he reddened. "Oh, you're right. I . . . I should go wash them off."

Paulie poured Mike a glass of club soda. "This should help get the stain out."

Mike mumbled a thanks as he backed away from Lucy. "I'll just . . . go and . . . take care of . . ." The sentence trailed off as he turned away, catching his uncle's eye and shooting him a questioning look before heading off.

"He's a funny chap," Lucy remarked. "Not at all the sort of man I'd have pictured Lucy marrying."

"Really, now. What kind of a fellow would you have pictured for your twin?"

Lucy shrugged. "Oh, someone flashy, dramatic, outrageous. Someone filled with self-importance."

"And how do you picture Mike?"

Lucy smiled. "You mean my first impression?"

Uncle Paulie chuckled. "Okay, sure. I'll play along. What's your first impression."

Lucy's expression turned contemplative. "Well, he's very nice looking. Low-key. Sweet. A bit innocent. Not that I think he's a pushover, mind you. No, I'd say he could be shrewd, strong-willed, even a bit stubborn at times." She paused, eyeing Uncle Paulie. "How am I doing so far?"

He grinned. "Honey, you're doing just fine."

"Is he still . . . in love with her? Lucy?"

Paulie raised his hands. "I don't think it's my place to tell you that. Stick around and you might get the answer out of Mikey, though."

"I will stick around for a bit. I'm hoping that Mike will help me reunite with my sister. Since I'm new in town, I could also use a friend. Mike seems . . . the friendly type."

Uncle Paulie folded his arms across his broad chest, his brown eyes sparkling with amusement. "I want you to know, kid, I'm on your side."

Lucy was sorely tempted to reveal the truth to Uncle Paulie, but couldn't risk it. Not that she thought he'd give her away. She knew that anything that would bring her back together with Mike would be A-OK with Uncle Paulie. But if she was going to carry off this charade, she had to stay in character. And it would be hard with Uncle Paulie giving her a sly look every time Mike's back was turned. Like the sly look he was giving her now. She knew that, like Stephie, he was yet to be convinced that she really was Ellen Warner.

"I welcome your support, Paulie. I only wish Lucy could realize we're on the same side. If only she hadn't run off like she did."

Uncle Paulie grinned broadly. "Yeah, a real shame she takes off just when you show up." He motioned to a stool. "Park it, kid. What'll ya have? Bourbon on the rocks? Or white-wine spritzer, easy on the spritz?"

"Just the spritz if you don't mind, Paulie. I don't imbibe."

"Whatever you say." He felt the need to repeat it as he filled a glass with seltzer for her. "Whatever you say."

She smiled. "I know what you're thinking, Paulie. Lucy's friend Stephie had much the same reaction when we met for lunch. She had a hard time believing I really am who I am."

He smiled facetiously as he set her glass on the bar in front of her. "What reaction? What's not to believe? You're Elaine, Lucy's twin sister—"

"Ellen. Ellen Katherine Warner." She dug into her purse and pulled out the fictitious McGurtry Foundation photo ID she'd had made that afternoon at some sleazy little print shop in lower Manhattan. The licentious master craftsman had even gone so far as to design a logo for the invented foundation. He'd charged a pretty penny for his little work of art. Lucy knew it was a definite extravagance, but it could be just the ticket to help her credibility.

She presented the official-looking plastic-coated card to Uncle Paulie. "I do so wish Lucy hadn't kept me such a deep, dark secret," she mused. "Why, anyone would think I had led some sort of shameful existence that couldn't be talked about in polite company. The truth is I've led a very dull, orderly, sedate life. I'm the cautious sort, always weighing the consequences, never wanting to take unwarranted risks. Lucy was the wild one, not me. Why, she'd do absolutely anything on a dare. The stories I could tell you. And her ex-husband. But I imagine since he was married to her for a brief time, he's experienced Lucy's wild side."

As she talked in her proper British accent she watched Uncle Paulie studying her ID. She could see the shadow of doubt cross his face and hid a smile by taking a sip of her "spritz." What she wouldn't do for a stiff shot of bourbon right about now.

Paulie tapped the card and then handed it back to her. This time, as he eyed her, his gaze was less suspicious, more curious.

She smiled. "We aren't identical twins, but we used to look very much alike when we were tots. I envied Lucy her golden hair and incredible green eyes, though."

Paulie's continued study started to unnerve her. She looked toward the men's room. "Do you suppose Mike is having some difficulty?"

Paulie grinned. "Knowing Mike, I'd say you could count on it."

"Oh, dear. I do feel responsible. He mightn't have knocked over the soda pop if I hadn't—"

"No, don't be silly. Mike's just a little clumsy. Part of his charm." Paulie slapped his hands down on the bar. "I'll go see if he needs some help."

MIKE WAS STANDING IN his boxer shorts holding his sopping-wet trousers under the electric hand-dryer when Paulie walked into the rest room.

"I got the stain out, but I can't go out there with a big wet spot," Mike muttered, glancing over at his uncle. "So, what do you think?"

"I don't know," Paulie said in a puzzled tone of voice. "At first I could have sworn it was Lucy. I mean, a gal can change the color of her hair, even her eyes—with contact lenses. And the accent. Lucy did grow up in London and even though she pretty much did away with her accent, she'd have no trouble recreating it. Still . . ." He scratched his forehead.

"Still what?" Mike urged.

"There's something different about her. And she's got this legitimate-looking company ID card." Paulie grinned. "Let me tell you. If Lucy ever took a picture that looked that bad she'd have burned it. This . . . Ellen . . . didn't even comment about it being a lousy shot."

"Then you believe she is Lucy's twin sister?" Mike asked.

"I don't know," Paulie said slowly, his gaze drifting to his nephew's pants which were starting to steam. He pulled them away from the dryer. Too late. The wet spot had become a large, telltale scorch mark.

Mike stared forlornly at his ruined trousers. "Now what do I do? I can't very well put them on and walk out there. What'll people think? What'll she think? If it's Lucy, she'll get a big laugh, all right. Call it a gut feeling, Uncle Paulie. I'm almost positive that woman out there is Lucy. After all, I was married to her for almost a year. She's up to something. I'm just not sure what it is."

"You really have nothing to lose by playing along," Paulie pointed out philosophically.

Mike frowned. "I'm not exactly up for being played for a fool—if that's what she's got in mind."

"You think she'd really sink that low?"

There was a glint in Mike's eye. "There's nothing I wouldn't put past my ex-wife."

A customer stepped into the men's room. He gave Mike and Paulie a nervous look, reminding Mike he was standing there in his boxer shorts. Mike hurriedly pulled on his trousers as the man stepped into one of the cubicles.

"I've got to go home and change. You'll have to . . . look after her, Uncle Paulie. I'll slip out the back door."

"You *are* going to come back, Mikey?"

"Of course, I'm going to come back. I'll play along with Lucy. At least, she'll think I'm playing along. But I plan to throw her a few curveballs when she least expects them."

"I don't know, Mikey. You may be getting in here over your head."

"And how is that?"

"There is the remote possibility that gal out there really is Lucy's twin sister," Paulie reminded him.

"I figure by the end of the evening I'll know for sure," Mike said with an air of confidence. "And if it is Lucy out there, mark my words, Uncle Paulie, she's not going to be the one to get the last laugh. Not after I give her a taste of her own medicine."

Mike's uncle smiled. "You know, Mikey, for a kid who's always trying so hard to be down-to-earth, sensible, and all that 'bloody rot' as they say in Merry Old England, you've got quite a sense of humor."

Mike winked. "Exactly what I'm going to demonstrate to Lucy."

LUCY HAD PLANTED HERSELF right outside the men's room so that when Mike stepped out, he practically walked straight into her.

"Oh, I'm sorry," he muttered, reddening as he saw her gaze drop to his trousers.

"What a shame," Lucy said.

"I'm afraid I'll have to catch a cab home and change," Mike mumbled.

"Would it be all right if I came with you?" Lucy asked in her most ingenuous voice. "I'm afraid lolling about a pub isn't exactly my cup of tea." She looked over at Paulie, who had followed Mike out. "No offense meant. It's a lovely pub, but I feel rather out of place." As she spoke, a shapely blonde in a skimpy teal-blue minidress passed by on her way to the ladies' room. "And overdressed," she added, still wearing her frumpy gray business suit.

Mike grinned. "Sure, Ellen. I'd love to take you home with me. We can get better acquainted that way."

Lucy was a bit taken aback when he swung an arm around her shoulder. Wasn't he being a bit overfamiliar with a woman he had never even met before? Or was he still having doubts that she was "Ellen"? Lucy smiled to herself. Yes, that was it, she decided. Well, the night was young.

"YOUR FLAT'S VERY LOVELY," Lucy said as Mike flicked on the light in the entryway. This was her first visit to his bachelor pad and she wasn't surprised to find the small living room neat as a pin, functional, and decorated in a simple, traditional style. She was sure that there were no dirty dishes stacked in his kitchen sink and that in his bedroom his bed was made, with not even an errant sock lying about on the floor.

"A far cry from the garish place I shared with Lucy," Mike commented, as he ushered her into the living room.

"Garish? Yes, I'm not surprised. Lucy never did have very refined taste. Her theory used to be that if it cost a lot, it must be tasteful."

Mike smiled. "A theory that she's held in good stead." As he spoke he came up behind her, placing his hands on her shoulders. "Here, let me help you off with your jacket. I want you to feel completely comfortable."

"Oh, well . . . that's very kind of you," Lucy said, feeling uneasy as he assisted her out of her suit jacket. It was one thing if he still thought she was Lucy and was trying to call her bluff. But, what if he did believe she was Ellen? Oh, sure, her goal was to get him interested in her, even make him fall head over heels in love with her. But she didn't expect it to be so easy. It upset her to think he would be putty in another woman's hands so soon after the two of them had spent that passionate night together. And all those passionate nights when they were married.

Mike's fingers glided down the silky sleeve of Lucy's blouse. Then he took hold of her hand and led her over to the couch. "Sit down, Ellen. Make yourself at home. I'll just run into the bedroom and change into something more comfortable."

He crossed over to the bedroom, leaving the door partly open. Her jaw dropped when Mike appeared at his bedroom door. He was wearing a silk paisley robe that had his monogram on the rolled collar—the one she'd given him for his last birthday. It matched the one he'd given her on her last birthday.

Lucy popped up from the sofa.

Giving no explanation for his attire, Mike sauntered over to his stereo. He placed a Barry Manilow disc in his CD player. Lucy was not a Manilow fan.

"Oh, Barry Manilow," she murmured. "One of my favorites."

Mike smiled. "Somehow, I guessed that."

"You . . . did?"

"Lucy can't stand him, you know."

"I didn't know," Lucy lied. "But I'm not surprised. When we were teens she was very big on punk rock. I detest punk rock."

"Mmm," he said, sauntering in her direction now. "So do I."

"Really?" she said, as he drew her into his arms.

"Shall we dance?" he said with a seductive lilt.

"Oh, I'm a terrible dancer. Really, two left feet. Lucy was the one who took the tap and ballet. I took piano." She stumbled into his arms.

"Lucy danced okay. But she was so showy," Mike said, smiling as he felt his dance partner stiffen in his arms. "I suppose some early childhood sense of inadequacy made her feel that she had to be the center of attention. Tell me, Ellen, was she always jealous of you?"

Lucy came to a dead stop. "Jealous? Of me? Why? She was so much prettier and livelier. So much more popular."

"My guess is you were the one who always did better in school, won the respect of your elders and your peers. You were the accomplished one. Am I right, Ellen?" He looked deep into her eyes.

"Yes . . . I suppose." Lucy lowered her lids, afraid he'd detect the contact lenses even though she'd taken the precaution of choosing pink-tinted lenses for her new gold frames. Meanwhile, her mind was in turmoil. Was Mike coming on to her, Lucy, or her, Ellen?

Mike, convinced it was Lucy in his arms, was just getting warmed up. "Funny, how two people can meet and something just . . . clicks. Has that ever happened to you, Ellen?" He began maneuvering her tense body around the floor again as Manilow began a new love song.

"Not . . . not really. That is . . . I do find you . . . very attractive, Mike. Compared to Lucy, I suppose, I must seem very . . . plain and dull to you."

"Plain? Dull? Oh, Ellen, if only Lucy could have been a little plainer, a little duller . . ."

Lucy's head jerked up. "What?"

"Oh, no, you don't understand. What I meant to say is that Lucy was more than I could cope with. So unpredictable, always flying off the handle at the least provocation, spending money like it grew on trees. Why, she felt she had to make a fashion statement even when she was vacuuming, which, believe me, she didn't do very often."

"Yes, well, she never did care for housework," Lucy muttered.

"Whereas you, Ellen . . . Well, you just seem so down-to-earth. You have an inner beauty that Lucy lacked. Vanity can do ugly things to a woman, don't you think?"

Lucy pressed her head to his shoulder, afraid her outraged expression would instantly give her away.

Mike wondered how much longer Lucy could keep her temper under wraps. He expected the china to start flying any minute. For once, he wouldn't mind.

Lucy had to know for sure just which one of her personas Mike was seducing. And there was only one way to find out. She gently edged away from Mike. "The collar on this blouse is a bit tight. You wouldn't get the wrong idea if I . . ." Her fingers went to the button at her collar, but Mike got there ahead of her.

"Here, let me. Sometimes those tiny pearl buttons can be tricky."

Lucy angled herself toward the light as Mike began tending to those "tricky" buttons. First one, then two, then three—

He stopped cold after undoing the third button, his gaze fixing on a small purple birthmark just above Lucy's right breast. Only Lucy didn't have a birthmark just above her right breast. That could only mean—

Oh, my God! Mike thought. *It's not Lucy!* He was seducing Lucy's twin sister, Ellen. A perfect stranger. What must she think of him? He knew what she thought—she thought he was attracted to her. And she was acting very much like she was attracted to him.

"What is it, Mike? Is there something wrong?" Lucy said innocently.

"Wrong? Wrong? No. No, no. Nothing's wrong. It's . . . I feel dizzy."

"Dizzy? Maybe you'd like to lie down."

"Lie down?"

"In your bed. You could be coming down with something."

"Coming down with something? Oh, yes. Yes, you're right, Ellen. You're absolutely right. I must be coming down with something." He stepped away from her. "I could be contagious. I would feel just awful if you got what I've got."

"Oh, I don't know. It might not be so awful."

"Oh, but it could be. It could be."

She smiled and stepped toward him. "Nonsense, love. You don't look that sick. Just pale. Maybe you had a few too many drinks before I arrived at your uncle's pub." She took a firm grip of his arm, her silk blouse still revealing creamy cleavage and the purple birthmark that Mike couldn't keep his eyes off.

"Come on, love. I'm going to tuck you into bed and make sure you have everything you need to make you feel better."

"Oh, Ellen, Ellen, that's very kind of you. I really feel so...embarrassed. I might have had a few too many," he lied. "I don't usually act the way I... What I'm trying to say is... You're a very sweet woman, Ellen, and I should never have... come on to you the way I did."

"Oh, but you did it very nicely, Mike."

"I did?"

"My feelings would be hurt if I thought it really was only the booze that made you so... friendly. Because something did happen when I first saw you, Mike. Something did click."

"It did?"

"Yes, love. It did. I think we have a great deal in common, Mike."

The biggest thing they had in common, Mike thought, was Lucy. What would Lucy think if she found out he'd come on to her twin sister? After knowing her for all of five minutes, no less. What chance would they ever have of reconciling? And yet if he told Ellen the truth, she'd be devastated. And Lucy would be furious at him for hurting her sister. She'd accuse him of being cruel, insensitive, devious. What a mess he'd made of everything. If only he'd trusted Lucy more.

Then he wouldn't have suspected her of pulling such a cheap trick.

"Ellen?"

"Yes, Mike?"

"Ellen, could I get you a cab to take you back to your hotel?"

"I thought . . . you liked me, Mike."

"Like you? Of course, I like you. Ellen, I . . . I like you. That's why . . . why I'm sending you home. I mean, to your hotel." He raced over to the phone and called for a cab, thrilled to learn one could be right over.

He returned to the woman he was now convinced was Ellen, and took hold of her hand. "Ellen, I want us to be . . . friends. I know you came here to work things out with Lucy and I . . . I'd like to help if I can. Of course, Lucy and I are estranged, but maybe if we put our heads together . . ."

Lucy smiled. "I'd like that, Mike."

He ushered her to the door, snatching up her jacket on the way. He helped her into it and then she turned to face him. "I'm glad you're not still my brother-in-law, Mike."

He smiled awkwardly, opening the door. But she made no move to leave. Mike leaned over to give her a brotherly peck on the cheek goodbye, but Lucy was quick to shift just enough for the kiss to land right on her lips.

Mike drew back. "Ellen, I hope I didn't give you the wrong impression."

"Believe me, Mike, you didn't. I'm very flattered." She wiped a trace of lipstick off his lips. "I do need a friend in town. And I appreciate the way you reached out to me. I can't imagine how Lucy could have let you go." She smiled. "But then, Lucy often didn't know a good thing when she had it. Don't you agree, love?"

"Well . . . I . . . I think you'd better hurry on down to the lobby. Your cab will be waiting."

She pressed her hand to his cheek. "Good night, Mike. I'll phone you in the morning to see how you're feeling. If that's okay with you?"

"Oh, sure. Sure, that's okay. That's great."

"This is my first time in New York. If you're feeling better, maybe you could even show me a few of the sights. And we can spend some of the day or evening putting our heads together to figure out what to do about Lucy."

Mike nodded dumbly. What to do about Lucy? That was the question, all right.

8

TEN MINUTES LATER the cab deposited Lucy, not at the Barkley Hotel where she'd booked a room under the name Ellen Warner for authenticity, but at the Harkness Towers. The doorman opened the door for her, but gave her a close scrutiny.

"Can I help you, miss?"

Lucy smiled, having forgotten for a moment that she was still "Ellen". "Oh, I'm Lucy Warner's sister." She quickly whipped out her phony ID.

"I'll just buzz her apartment and let her know you're on your way up then, Miss Warner," Allan, the doorman, said politely.

"Oh, don't bother. I . . . uh . . . left her at the party we were at." Again she dug her hand into her purse. "She gave me the key." She held it up for the doorman's inspection.

He smiled. "I have to be careful, you understand, Miss Warner. But it's pretty obvious you two are sisters, though. Why, without the glasses, and with your hair a shade lighter and worn more in your sister's style, you two would look almost like identical twins."

Lucy grinned. "We *are* twins. Unfortunately for me, not identical."

The doorman flushed. "Oh, I didn't mean . . . "

Lucy gave him a pat on the shoulder. "That's all right. Glamour isn't everything."

Just as Lucy started to cross the lobby, she heard familiar voices behind her. Another opportunity to put "Ellen" to the test.

"Evening, ladies. And how was your bingo game tonight?"

"Simply dreadful, Allan," Clara Ponds announced to the doorman. "As I told Eunice, we ought to be doing better things with our money than gambling."

"It isn't really gambling," Eunice Blanford argued. "The money we lost does go to the church, after all. And they, in turn, use it to do good deeds for those less fortunate—"

"If we keep losing money the way we did tonight, we'll be two of 'those less fortunate,'" Clara said snippily.

The elderly pair met up with Lucy at the elevator. Clara was somewhat circumspect in her study, but Eunice was not one for subtleties.

"Is it you, Lucy?" Eunice asked point-blank, her tone puzzled. Why, she wondered, would such a beautiful woman undergo such a transformation unless she had gone to a costume party or some such thing?

Lucy acknowledged the question with a faint shake of her head. "I'm Lucy's sister, Ellen, from London."

Clara eyed her suspiciously. "Lucy never mentioned she had a sister."

"Oh. Are you good friends, then?" Lucy asked guilelessly.

"Well, really," the ever-honest Eunice confessed, "I believe she's a bit miffed at us at the moment. Not that we didn't apologize. To her husband, as well. I should say her ex-husband. It isn't that we thought him a likely wife murderer. He certainly doesn't look or act like one. Oh, no. Just the opposite."

"Which is precisely the point," Clara said starchily as the elevator arrived. "It's the ones that look innocent whom you have to watch out for. Personally, I think Lucy should be very grateful to us."

"Oh, I think she is grateful," Eunice said as all three women stepped into the elevator. "Underneath. Still, no one likes to see someone they love about to be arrested for murder."

"If she loved him she wouldn't have divorced him. Besides, he was not about to be arrested," Clara argued. "The police were simply following up a lead."

"Our lead. A mistaken one, I'm sorry to say," Eunice murmured, casting a slightly accusatory look at her companion.

Clara dismissed the look and focused on Lucy's "Ellen." "Are you staying with Lucy?"

"I was just dropping by," Lucy said, deciding it would be best not to stray too much from her story in case The Odd Couple ran into Mike. "I'm booked at a hotel. Actually, I haven't seen Lucy for years."

Eunice peered closer. "There's a definite resemblance."

"Well, of course there's a resemblance," Clara said brusquely. "They're sisters."

The elevator came to a stop at the fourteenth floor. Clara stepped out, but Eunice lingered for a moment. "Do tell Lucy when you see her that we really are most sorry. Now that we're confident Mike isn't . . . dangerous, we do wish they'd get back together again."

"Eunice," Clara said sharply, having to press the elevator button to keep the door from closing.

Eunice ignored her companion. "Oh, there were fireworks between those two, but I find fireworks quite exciting, don't you?"

Lucy squeezed the old woman's hand. "Yes, love. I do adore fireworks."

PAULIE WAS SURPRISED by Mike's solo appearance back at the club later that night. Mike headed straight for his uncle's back-room office. He was already stretched out on the worn green plastic couch, one arm slung over his forehead, when Paulie walked in.

"Something tells me things didn't go too well," Paulie said, a touch of humor in his voice.

Mike found nothing amusing about his uncle's talent for understatement. "It was a disaster. I can't believe the way I behaved. I can't imagine what she must think of me."

Paulie pulled up a chair close to the couch. "Lucy?"

Mike lowered his arm from his face. One bloodshot eye was visible. "Lucy? No. Ellen."

"Ellen? Mikey. . . ."

"I know. I know. I was so damn sure it was Lucy."

"So, what changed your mind? It must have been something pretty convincing."

Mike groaned, covering his one visible eye again with his arm. "Do you have any aspirin around, Uncle Paulie? I've got a splitting headache."

Paulie tugged his nephew's hand away from his face. "Tell Uncle Paulie all about it."

Mike rolled over onto his side. "Forget the aspirin. How about some bromo for my stomach?"

"Come on, kid. How bad could it have been?"

Mike lifted his head up a few inches from the sofa. "I seduced Lucy's twin sister. I had her half undressed before I realized—" He dropped his head back down on the sofa and groaned again.

Paulie patted his nephew on the back. "A large bromo coming up."

LUCY WAS SURROUNDED by a pile of layouts in her office the next morning when Stephie popped in.

"Hey, you were supposed to call me last night and tell me how things went. So, did he fall for it? Did he believe you were Ellen? What happened?" Stephie questioned in typical rapid-fire fashion.

A weariness suffused Lucy. "I wish I knew what happened. I've been trying to sort it all out. I can't be sure, though."

Stephie pulled up a seat and plucked a layout sheet from Lucy's hand. "Okay, we'll take it one step at a time. When he first saw you, what was his reaction?"

"He spilled a glass of cola all over his trousers."

Stephie laughed. "That's good, right? That means he was shook. Really shook. Because I was shook and I didn't spill anything over myself."

"True," Lucy muttered.

"Okay, and then? After he spilled the drink on his trousers?" Stephie prodded.

"He burned them," she said deadpan.

"Burned them?"

"Oh, it doesn't matter. The long and the short of it is, he took me home with him and tried to get me into bed."

Stephie's mouth dropped open. "He did?"

"No, he didn't," Lucy said forlornly. "That is, he didn't succeed. He got cold feet at the last minute."

"Who did he get cold feet with?" Stephie demanded. "Who did he seduce? Who did he think you were? Lucy or Ellen?"

Lucy wasn't listening. "I'd like to think it was the birthmark that stopped him, but I'm just not sure."

Stephie sank into a chair. "You're going too fast for me. What birthmark?"

"Ellen's birthmark. A little purple blotch over her right breast. I thought if things eventually got that far, Ellen ought to have some distinguishing mark."

"Very clever," Stephie said, her voice touched with admiration.

Lucy's expression was mournful. "Only I never dreamed things would go so far so fast. And the things Mike said about me . . ."

"What did he say?" Stephie asked eagerly.

"Oh . . . awful things. I thought at first he knew it was me and that's why he was saying them. What if I'm wrong? What if he's right? Maybe I am all those things. Maybe Ellen is more his type. That was the point of all this, anyway, wasn't it? I suppose I should be happy that Mike and Ellen clicked. If they did click." Her voice lacked conviction.

"Lucy, you're driving me crazy."

"What's driving me crazy," Lucy said with a sigh, "is that I always thought I understood Mike, knew just what was going on in that tidy, orderly mind of his. I can't believe he would have seduced a woman who was a perfect stranger, never mind that she was my twin sister. And he did come to a dead stop when he saw that birthmark. So, he must have thought it was me and not Ellen up to then and was just turning the tables on me, trying to make me jealous. But then again, he might have been bowled over by her and realized once he'd gotten me—her, "Ellen"—half undressed, that he was moving too fast."

Lucy stood and started to pace. "What gets me is, if he did think I was Ellen, he certainly made a faster move on her than he did on me when we first met. He certainly didn't lose control—or almost lose control—on our first date."

Stephie broke out in a broad smile. "I don't believe it. You're jealous of her. You're jealous of Ellen. You're going nuts over a woman you invented. You're going nuts over you."

Lucy frowned. "It isn't me. Not the real me."

"Wasn't the whole point to prove to Mike that Ellen could be the real you? You were the one who said he'd be more attracted to Ellen."

Lucy's frown deepened. "I know that. I guess in a way I was hoping—"

"Hoping that he really wouldn't fall for her?"

"I'm not making any sense, am I?"

Stephie grinned. "Women in love rarely make any sense." She walked over to Lucy. "How about coming over for dinner tonight? Jerry's out of town on business. I'll tuck Amy in early and we'll stuff our faces and sort it all out."

"I can't. I've got a date. With Mike." Lucy could only manage a wilted smile. "That is, Ellen has a date. She's meeting him at the Empire State Building at three."

"The Empire State Building?"

"He's going to show my twin sister the sights."

"IT'S REALLY A GREAT view," Mike said. "When it isn't foggy. You must be used to fog."

Lucy's expression was blank.

"London?" Mike prodded.

"Oh, right," she replied. "London. It's always bloody foggy in London."

"By the way, I gave Stephie a buzz earlier," Mike said in as casual a tone as he could muster. "Just to see when Lucy was getting back. She wasn't sure." He hesitated. "You haven't heard from her yourself, have you?"

"From Stephie?"

"No. No, Lucy. She hasn't written or phoned you or anything?"

"Actually, she did send a note to my hotel."

"She did? What did she say?"

"She agreed to a meeting. She invited me to come out to the place she's staying at in Long Island for the weekend. I believe it's East Hampton."

"She did? That's great. That's what you wanted, isn't it?" he added when he saw that Ellen didn't seem very enthused about the invitation.

"Oh, it is. It's just that things seem more complicated now." She eyed Mike, reaching for his hand. "I was thinking that we might have this weekend to get to know each other better."

"Ellen. About last night . . ."

"Yes, Mike. What about it?"

He was stymied where to go from there. If he was too apologetic, she'd be insulted. If he didn't apologize, he'd be leading her on.

She smiled. "It's okay, Mike. I was flattered. I never thought that a man who knew my beautiful and glamorous sister so intimately would ever even notice I existed."

Mike felt like an absolute heel. "You shouldn't feel that way about yourself, Ellen. You're attractive, bright, clear-headed . . ."

"I don't feel particularly clear-headed around you, Mike," she said.

"Ellen, can I ask you something?"

"Anything, Mike."

"What did the two of you have a falling-out about? You and Lucy."

Lucy compressed her lips.

"I'm sorry," Mike said softly. "It's really none of my business."

Lucy reached out and took hold of his hand. "I don't mind telling you, Mike. I usually have difficulty opening up to people. It's different with you."

Mike smiled awkwardly.

"It was over a bloke."

"A bloke?"

"You know. A young man. He was studying to be a barrister. I was wildly in love with him. And I thought he was in love with me. Until he set eyes on Lucy. She stole him right out from under me. Well, not literally, if you know what I mean."

Mike looked away, embarrassed. "Yes."

"We fought bitterly, Lucy and I. I called her spiteful, irresponsible, inconsiderate, selfish, vain. Having known Lucy as well as you did, I gather you know what I mean. Something tells me she hasn't changed all that much."

"Well, Lucy can be . . ."

Lucy gripped his arm. "It's all right, Mike. I'm sure, like . . . like David . . . you were taken in by her beauty, her wit, her charm, her . . . insouciance."

"Who's David?"

"The bloke."

"Oh. What happened with David and Lucy?"

"That's the rub. Nothing. She lured him in, grew quickly bored, and tossed him overboard with nary a thought. That was when we had the worst of our blowup."

"Maybe she realized they just weren't right for each other."

"You're sweet, Mike. But something tells me she did much the same to you as she did to David. And all I can say about that is that I think Lucy's a fool."

"She's not a fool, Ellen. And it isn't true that she grew bored and dumped me."

"Why did you break up, then?"

"Well . . . There isn't a simple answer to that question, really."

"Oh, Mike, you're such a dear man. I know you don't want to speak ill of my sister. I truly admire you for that."

"It wasn't all Lucy's fault, Ellen. I can be trying at times. I'm a stickler for neatness—"

"Neatness is next to godliness in my book, Mike."

"And I'm always watching every penny—"

"You mean Lucy spent excessive amounts of money. No doubt on frivolous trinkets and costumes."

"'Excessive' might be too strong—"

"I'm a great believer in the motto, A Penny Saved Is A Penny Earned. Don't you agree?"

"Well . . . yes."

Lucy smiled. "It's very nice being up here on the Empire State Building with you, Mike. Even in the fog."

After the Empire State Building they toured the New York Stock Exchange. Lucy's choice. At least, she thought it would be something "Ellen" would choose. Dinner was at an inexpensive little café in SoHo. Again, "Ellen's" choice. Lucy wanted to show Mike that she didn't need to frequent fancy, expensive restaurants.

"Ellen" spent most of the dinner encouraging Mike to talk about his work. Lucy believed that she had been lax in that area, always going on in the past about the ups and downs of the modeling agency, but never spending enough time asking Mike about his day—his triumphs, his problems.

Although Mike got a lot of satisfaction out of being a successful accountant with one of the biggest firms in Manhattan, discussing his work in his view made for very dry conversation. It had always pleased him to hear Lucy go on about the agency. She was so dramatic, such a wonderfully animated storyteller, always finding some anecdote that would make him laugh.

He tried to steer the conversation around to "Ellen," politely asking her about her work, her life. Her account was even duller than his. She spoke about social responsibility, business ethics, effective management, and what she described as the agony and ecstasy of corporate life. Mike found it agony to pretend to be interested, but he was determined not to be rude. He marveled that twins could be so dissimilar.

When he brought "Ellen" back to her hotel later that night, he asked her if she was going to see Lucy in the Hamptons.

"What do you think I should do, Mike?"

"I think you should go. In fact, I was thinking . . ." He hesitated.

"What were you thinking, Mike?"

"I was thinking that maybe I ought to go along with you."

"Oh, no. I don't think that would be a good idea at all."

"You don't?" Mike said, disappointed. He'd hoped that if he could help bring Lucy and Ellen together, it would prove to Lucy that he still cared.

She kissed him lightly on the lips. "I'll see you when I get back on Monday and tell you all about it."

"Okay. Give her my best, though, will you?"

She gave him a curious smile. "You're very nice to a woman who divorced you."

He shrugged awkwardly. As he turned to go, she called out to him: "Mike, you do like me, don't you? You're not just being kind to me because I'm sort of . . . family?"

It was one of those loaded questions. "No. I do like you, Ellen. What's . . . not to like?"

They both smiled uneasy smiles.

LATER THAT NIGHT, MIKE showed up at Paulie's Greenwich Village apartment a couple of blocks from the club.

"I was driving by in a cab and saw that your lights were still on."

Paulie pulled him inside the door. "You look like hell."

"I don't know what to do, Uncle Paulie. I want Lucy, only somehow I've gotten Ellen instead."

"Ellen's not bad, Mikey."

"No, she's fine. She's everything Lucy isn't. Everything I always harped on Lucy to be. Ellen's sensible, practical, conscientious, attentive . . ."

"So, what's the problem?"

Mike wandered into his uncle's galley kitchen, opened the fridge, stared inside at the mostly empty shelves and closed the door.

"You want me to send out for a pizza? You hungry, Mikey?"

"I'm starved, Uncle Paulie," he said dramatically, resting his heated forehead against the cool refrigerator door. "I'm starved for Lucy. I can't get her out of my mind. The more time I spend with Ellen, the more I think about Lucy, about what we had, about how exciting life was with her."

He squeezed by his uncle and went into the small, cluttered living room. Usually the clutter bothered him. Tonight he didn't even notice it.

"I've got to tell you, Uncle Paulie. Ellen's a nice woman and all, but the truth is, she's painfully dull. And you know what I keep thinking?"

"No, kid. What do you keep thinking?"

Mike tossed a magazine off the cushion of a recliner and sank down into it. "I keep thinking that I'm a lot like Ellen. Which means Lucy must have found me just as painfully dull as I find her twin. Dull, tedious, penny-pinching, starchy... We make quite a pair, Ellen and I. A perfect match," he said sardonically.

Paulie smiled sympathetically. "That's just one side of you, Mikey. You may not know it, kid, but you've got some of your mama's genes in you and she was a pretty wild, irrepressible spirit in her heyday."

"She was?"

"And your dad may have been a bum, but I gotta tell ya, he was a charming bum. Charmed the pants right off—" Uncle Paulie flushed. "You know what I mean, kid."

"I know what you mean, Uncle Paulie. But I think those genes got lost somewhere down the road."

"Baloney. You've got what it takes. You just need—" Paulie stopped abruptly, his eyes widening, the tip of his tongue gliding thoughtfully over his upper lip.

Mike observed him closely. "What? What do I need, Uncle Paulie?"

Paulie rubbed his palms together gleefully. "Yes, sirree, I think I've got it. By George, I've got it," Paulie said in a New York version of a British accent.

"What? What?" Mike said impatiently as he leaned forward.

Paulie's eyes positively glinted with mischief. "What you need, kid, is to track down that dashing, debonair kid brother of yours."

"What dashing, debonair kid brother? What brother?"

Paulie cupped his chin and gave Mike a long, close study.

"What are you cooking up, Uncle Paulie?" Mike asked warily.

"Why not, Mikey? Lucy has this dull, plain-Jane sister she never talked about. Why couldn't you have a kid brother who was, say, the black sheep in the family that you never discussed?"

"There's one big difference between Lucy's sister and my brother, Uncle Paulie. Ellen is real . . . and my black-sheep brother isn't."

But Paulie wasn't listening. "Name. We need a good name. Something suave but offbeat. Rugged, a little dangerous—"

"You mean you want me to play this suave, rugged, dangerous kid brother? Forget it, Uncle Paulie. I could never pull it off. Lucy would see right through me in two minutes flat."

"Trey!"

Mike squinted. "What?"

"The name, Mikey. Trey. Trey Austin Powell."

"You're kidding."

"What do ya mean? It's perfect. Lucy will love it."

"You're crazy, Uncle Paulie."

Paulie chuckled. "Crazy like a fox."

"Even if I could pull something like that off—which I couldn't," Mike said emphatically, "what's the point?"

"The point? The point? Kid, where's your head? Put on your thinking cap. Lucy meets Trey, this devil-may-care version of you. She falls head over heels in love with him, telling him he's everything she always wanted and then—voilà— she finds out in the end that he's really you, the husband she was so convinced was dull, tedious, penny-pinching. You'll get to show her this whole other side of you, Mikey. It'll give her the opportunity, firsthand to see what a wild, exciting guy you really are."

"But I'm not a wild, exciting guy."

Paulie winked. "You will be, kid. When I get through with you."

9

"Now I know how Audrey Hepburn felt," Mike grumbled.

"What do you mean?" Paulie asked, popping another videocassette into his player. It was after hours at the club and the two men had the place to themselves.

"In *My Fair Lady*. When Rex Harrison tried to turn her from a cockney flower vendor into a princess."

"And he succeeded, right?"

"It's no use, Uncle Paulie. You've made me sit through a half-dozen films starring Cary Grant, Clark Gable—"

"Don't forget Errol Flynn. A touch of swashbuckler and a touch of class is a *supremo* combination, kid."

"But when I try to mimic them I feel more like Woody Allen."

Paulie chuckled. "You're being too hard on yourself, Mikey. We've only begun."

"No, Uncle Paulie. I'm quitting," Mike said, spinning away from the bar on his stool and then getting off.

"Quitting?" Paulie clicked off the video player. "Sure, okay. Hey, if you can't cut the mustard, kid . . ."

Mike shrugged.

"Maybe winning Lucy back isn't all that important to you."

Mike turned to his uncle. "That isn't fair. I don't want to make a complete fool of myself, that's all."

"What if I wager you five hundred—no, make that five thousand smackeroos—that you can pull it off?" Paulie's hand remained poised on the remote control for the VCR.

"By watching all these films and trying to mimic those actors?"

"This is just the beginning of the crash course, Mikey. Lesson number one."

"What's lesson number two?" Mike asked warily.

Paulie grinned.

MIKE STARED AT HIMSELF in the mirror, his expression grim.

"I can't breathe in these jeans," Mike complained. "They're two sizes too small and they look like someone else has worn them for a couple of years."

The salesman, a pony-tailed young man in even tighter jeans and a red open-weave shirt that looked like it was made of fishnet, smiled. "That's the beauty of the line. Anyone can design a pair of jeans that look brand-new, but to make new jeans look worn—in just the right places—is an art. Nobody does it better than Roberto Colina."

Mike rolled his eyes. "Okay, what about a shirt?"

Uncle Paulie and the salesman shared a chuckle.

"Mikey, you're wearing a shirt," Paulie told him.

"I'm wearing an undershirt," Mike said.

The salesman was aghast. "Nobody calls the La Ferlia tank top an undershirt, my man."

Mike stared at the La Ferlia tank top in the mirror. They could give it any name they liked. To him this was a plain white undershirt. And like the jeans, a good two sizes too small. As an afterthought, he glanced at the price tag. And nearly passed out.

"La Ferlia is expensive," the salesman said blithely, "but worth every penny."

"Twelve thousand pennies?" Mike asked dryly.

"We've got a few Lewis Reeds around," the salesman said, his tone condescending. "They go for sixty to seventy-five bucks. But there's no comparison between a Reed and a La Ferlia."

Paulie squeezed Mike's bare shoulder and motioned to the salesman to take a hike.

"You look sexy as hell, kid."

"I feel naked."

"That's the idea."

"I couldn't walk out in public looking like this," Mike insisted, adding, "And I certainly couldn't *sit*."

"Sure, you could. The jeans will give once you've worn them for a while."

"And I don't care if this is a La Ferlia or a La Bamba, this is an undershirt. Almost identical to the ones you used to make me wear under my shirt when I was in grade school."

His uncle grinned. "Just think. If I'd only had you take the shirt off, you might be wearing a La Paulie now instead of a La Ferlia."

Mike continued studying his reflection in the mirror. "You can't tell me Cary Grant would have worn an outfit like this."

"No, but Clark Gable did. And all the popular young hunks do now."

"I've never thought of myself as a hunk type."

"Well, now you've got hunk written all over you. Besides, I bet that director dude Lucy dated owns a whole drawerful of La Ferlias."

"He probably does," Mike conceded. He turned sideways and then looked at his refection in the mirror head-on again. "You really think I look . . . sexy like this?"

"More to the point, I'm betting big bucks here that Lucy will."

Mike remained dubious.

"I know it's a little hard to get used to a new style, kid," Uncle Paulie cajoled. "Especially for a guy who's been stubbornly partial to nondescript blue suits for half his life. Trust me, wearing an outfit like this can really make you feel like a new man."

Mike sighed. "I guess you're right. I certainly don't feel like myself."

Paulie gave his nephew's shoulder a friendly jab. "Anyway, this is just the beginning. We need some classy evening clothes, a cashmere sweater or two—women go ape over cashmere."

"If an undershirt in this place costs one hundred and twenty dollars I'd hate to see the price tag on a cashmere sweater," Mike said mournfully.

"I thought you wanted to show Lucy you didn't spend every waking minute counting pennies. And believe me, a woman like Lucy will be able to tell a La Ferlia from a Lewis Reed."

"You're probably right," Mike relented.

Paulie motioned the salesman back. "Okay, now we put some zing into his evening attire."

Mike was too dazed to grumble when he was decked out in an Armani black spandex suit that actually stretched, matched with a multicolored vest, and a bird-patterned red, blue and black silk shirt. He did balk when the salesman suggested an African necklace made of bones instead of a necktie. Paulie took pity on him and nixed the necklace.

"WHAT DO YA MEAN, ya can't drive a motorcycle?"

"I mean, it's dangerous."

"What, dangerous? There's so much traffic in the city, ya can't go more than ten miles an hour on the thing."

"Uncle Paulie . . ."

"So, why did we buy those Ralph Lauren black leather pants?"

Mike grimaced. "Good question."

"Ya gotta rent the bike, kid. It's all part of the image."

"Well, one thing's for sure. Lucy will never suspect it's me if I pull up on a Harley-Davidson motorcycle."

Paulie gave his nephew a hearty slap on the back. "That's the ticket."

"Ticket. Right. I'll probably get some of those, too."

Paulie grinned. "Tell ya what I'll do. I'll pick up the tab if you get nailed by a cop."

"Okay, you win."

"No, you win," Paulie countered with a smile. "You win, kid. Five thousand bucks and the girl. Not bad winnings, if you ask me."

Mike didn't comment that the five thousand dollars would just make a dent in the bundle he was spending to turn himself into a "new man." Besides, the money really didn't matter. Mike knew, just as Uncle Paulie did, that the real prize he was after was Lucy.

After paying the one-month lease for the motorcycle, Mike thought the preparations were over. How wrong he was!

"NO WAY," MIKE SAID adamantly, rising from the elevated chair in the beauty salon. "I will not wear a wig and that's final."

The beautician, a pretty brunette, tried to explain. "It isn't a wig, honey. It's a fall." She leaned over him, her strong fruity perfume making Mike a little queasy. "See, what we're going to do is just weave the fall into your real hair to add a bit of length, give you a more arty look. The longer length is definitely in. And to be honest, honey, the clothes you're wearing and your 'do' don't jive."

Mike was wearing his newly purchased upmarket facsimile of work clothes—a close-fitting cotton shirt, a bandanna around his neck, and his too-tight jeans, hoping to stretch them a little. The outfit made him feel a little like Henry Fonda's Okie dust bowler in *The Grapes of Wrath*.

The beautician urged him back into the salon chair. Sitting was still uncomfortable. It was ironic, he thought, to own jeans that didn't give and evening clothes that did. Nothing made any sense to him anymore—least of all the notion of wearing a "wig."

But the beautician, goaded by Uncle Paulie, was already beginning the weaving process. Uncle Paulie held up a mirror behind Mike, urging him to watch the procedure closely so that he could imitate it whenever the situation called for Trey to be "reborn."

"This is going to give you that new Rough Chic look," the beautician assured Mike as her fingers busily worked their magic. "The color blend is perfect. Only your hairdresser and your uncle would ever know the truth."

"What do you suggest about his skin?" Uncle Paulie asked her.

"My skin?" Mike broke in anxiously. There was a limit here. . . .

"We want a shade that gives him a kind of Tahiti tan," Uncle Paulie said, ignoring Mike's question.

"Tahiti?" Mike turned to eye his uncle, but Cindy, the beautician, jerked his head back into position.

"You want a tropical-island tan," Cindy said contemplatively. "I think a blend of foundation and face powder—"

"Makeup?" Mike squealed. "You're talking makeup?"

"Relax, Mikey," Uncle Paulie soothed. "Actors wear makeup all the time."

"Onstage. In the movies. Not in real life," Mike argued. "I can't start wearing makeup."

Twenty minutes later, Mike stared at himself in the mirror. His dark hair was now nearly down to his shoulders and his face glowed with a healthy tan. Even he didn't recognize himself.

"I look like a jerk," Mike muttered.

"Lucy's gonna flip when she sees ya, Mikey," Paulie insisted.

"If she doesn't," Cindy said with a seductive smile, "you can always give my phone a jingle." She actually slipped a piece of paper with her phone number on it into Mike's shirt pocket.

DURING THE TWO WEEKS that Mike was in training to be Trey, he had another major dilemma to cope with—Ellen. After her trip to the Hamptons, she returned, telling him that she and Lucy had made some progress but they'd agreed to take it slow. This meant that Ellen had plenty of time to spend with Mike. One evening, Mike, dressed up as Trey, was practicing in the mirror.

"Lucy, Lucy, Lucy," he murmured in his best imitation of Cary Grant. "You are a dream come true, Lucy. The woman I've been searching for all my life. None of the women in Tahiti could hold a candle to your loveliness, Lucy."

He frowned at his reflection. Tahiti. Why had he let Uncle Paulie talk him into Tahiti? Because, as Uncle Paulie had insisted, Lucy had never been to Tahiti; Tahiti was exotic and romantic; and because it was just the place for a young artist to have run off to all those many years ago.

Mike's frown deepened. Artist. That was a laugh. He had trouble drawing stick figures. But Uncle Paulie had taken care of that, just as he'd seemingly taken care of all the other "minor details," as he'd put it. A musician buddy of Uncle Paulie's had an artist pal who was out of town for a few weeks. Paulie's buddy arranged for Mike—that is, Trey—to use the SoHo studio any time he wanted. The best part, Uncle Paulie had said, was that this artist even painted in the style of Gauguin, who actually had painted in Tahiti for years.

Mike saw that his frown lines had caked his makeup. Maybe he was putting it on too heavily. Just as he was smoothing it out with a tissue, feeling utterly ridiculous, his downstairs buzzer rang.

He blanched when he heard Ellen's voice. She was in the lobby, wanting to come up to his apartment for a few minutes. One thing he'd learned in the past couple of weeks about Ellen—it wasn't easy to dissuade her.

"Just...uh...give me a couple of minutes to get...decent," he muttered to her before clicking off. He felt a little like Superman, dashing into his bathroom to change back into Clark Kent before his doorbell rang.

Breathlessly, he opened the door on her fourth ring. "Ellen."

"Hi. I hope you don't mind my dropping in without calling first," Lucy said.

Mike shook his head. "No. No, it's just that I was ... working on some ... stuff." He tucked a loose tail of his blue-and-white pin-striped broadcloth shirt into his khaki trousers.

"Must have been dirty work," Lucy commented, rubbing off what she took for a dirt smudge from his jaw.

"Oh ... Uh ... yes. I was cleaning out my ... fireplace."

"Isn't it a bit warm out still to be thinking of fires?"

"Oh, well, I wasn't thinking of fires. It's just... Well, never put off today what you can do tomorrow. I mean, never put off tomorrow ..."

"You're awfully edgy tonight, Mike. Is something troubling you?"

"Troubling me? No. No, nothing's troubling me."

She smiled. "Because I want you to know, Mike, if there is ever anything troubling you in any way, any way at all, I hope you see me as the kind of person you could come to with your ... your troubles."

"I do, Ellen. I do see you as that kind of person."

"I suppose," she said, wandering into Mike's living room, "that Lucy wasn't exactly as receptive to your troubles as she might have been."

Mike followed her into the room, nervously glancing at the perfectly clean fireplace. "Oh, Lucy was receptive ... at times."

She glanced back at him. "Was she?"

"I suppose I wasn't really one to talk much about my ... troubles. It wasn't all Lucy's fault."

"So, you do have troubles."

"No. I just mean ... Ellen, would you like a drink? Some lemonade? Iced tea?" He felt so confused, so torn. After all, Ellen was everything he'd always wished Lucy would be. Was he just holding on to some romantic fantasy? Ellen really did seem to care for him. She had all the right qualities. He did admire her. And like her. She wasn't even unattractive—even if she did lack Lucy's dramatic beauty.

"Thank you, love. Lemonade would be lovely."

He hurried off into his tiny kitchen, only to find Ellen close on his heels.

"I left Lucy's place and I was thinking maybe we could talk for a while."

"You were with Lucy?" Mike stepped away from the refrigerator door, forgetting to take out the bottle of lemonade.

"Yes," she said, reaching in for it herself.

"How's she doing?" Mike asked in as casual a voice as he could muster.

"Oh, fine. She invited me to a gallery opening of some artist friend of hers tomorrow night." Lucy edged past Mike and removed two glasses from his cupboard.

Mike was about to suggest he accompany Ellen to the gallery opening, but then a much better idea hit him. "I was going to ask if I could come along, but I just remembered I've got a business dinner tomorrow night."

"I know you're not any crazier about art openings than I am. Especially the wild stuff Lucy's artist friends are into. I was going to suggest coming over here instead, tomorrow night. I could cook you a nice dinner and we could watch a video or something. I love to cook. And it's such a waste throwing money away on restaurants. They charge a bloody fortune and you never feel you get your money's worth."

Mike had to agree with her. Lucy certainly wouldn't have.

Lucy smiled, stepping closer to him, handing him a glass of lemonade. "That's what I like about you, Mike. A man with simple tastes and a good head on his shoulders."

Mike took a long swallow of his drink. Standing there in those tight quarters with Ellen made him feel very uneasy. He'd tried his best, after that disastrous first night, to slow things down between them, but he'd been kidding himself in trying to deny that Ellen was infatuated with him. She'd even gone so far as to delay her return to London indefinitely. Much to his dismay, it seemed the foundation she worked for was considering an adjunct office in Manhattan and the president had encouraged Ellen to stay as long as necessary to weigh the pros and cons. Mike was afraid that she might not only encourage the opening of a branch, but end up running it. If Ellen remained in Manhattan, how was he ever going to extricate himself? Was he absolutely certain he wanted to?

"Here, have some more," Lucy said, brushing up against him as she topped off his glass.

She caught Mike off guard and some of the drink splashed on her blouse as his hand tipped.

"Oh, Ellen. I'm sorry." Reflexively, he went to wipe off the liquid but it was right over her breast. He flashed on that birthmark again and pulled his hand back sharply.

"It's nothing," Lucy said, nonchalantly unbuttoning her blouse. "I'll just wash it off—" She stopped short, remembering she'd forgotten to paint on her purple birthmark. Clasping the front of her open blouse shut, she stepped back, bumping into the stove. "I'm . . . I'm sorry, Mike," she muttered. "I certainly don't want you to think I make a habit of . . . of undressing in front of every—"

"Oh, I don't think that at all. Believe me. And don't be sorry, Ellen. Really, there's nothing to be sorry about. I'm the one that's sorry. For spilling on you. It was so clumsy of me. I'll just . . . step out and finish up with . . . with the fireplace while you . . . uh . . . take care of your blouse."

"It isn't that I'm overly modest, Mike. It's just that . . ."

He was halfway out the kitchen door. "You don't have to explain, Ellen. I . . . I admire that in you."

"You do?"

"Yes. Modesty is very . . . admirable. I'm modest myself."

"Something else we share in common, then," Lucy said brightly.

Mike gave a wilted nod and made a hasty retreat.

A few minutes later Lucy returned to the living room. There was a damp spot on the front of her blouse. Mike tried not to notice.

"I've got the stain out. When this dries it will be good as new," Lucy said, curling up on the couch and patting the cushion next to her. "Come sit down, love."

Mike readjusted the screen in front of his fireplace and reluctantly took the seat beside her. "You said you just came from Lucy's place. How did things go?"

"Oh, I suppose they went okay. I just wish . . ."

"What do you wish, Ellen?"

"I wish the two of us had more in common. I can't imagine how the two of you lived together all those months, being so different from each other," Lucy said. *Liar!* She could imagine it only too well. There had been something appealing to her about the two of them being so different. It had generated excitement, surprise, even mystery. Yes, it had caused fireworks. And what wondrous displays they'd created sometimes. Lucy couldn't help wondering what life would be like with Mike, now that she was turning over this new leaf. Would there still be fireworks?

"They say opposites attract," Mike mused.

"Yes, they've got that saying in Jolly Old England, as well," Lucy murmured.

"Not that attraction should be the only basis for—"

"Oh, I quite agree," she said before he finished.

Mike stiffened as she rested her head on his shoulder. Lucy didn't notice. Being close to Mike like this brought back such vivid memories. How she missed the intimacy the two of them had shared. Since he'd left, she'd spent countless hours fighting off her longing for him, putting her desire on hold until she could win him back through "Ellen."

All Mike could think of, as Ellen snuggled up against him, were the many hours he'd spent with Lucy wrapped in his arms. A wave of longing washed over him. And guilt.

"Ellen . . ."

"Yes, Mike?"

When he didn't answer, she lifted her head up. "What is it, Mike?"

He kissed her chastely on the lips. "We'd better call it a night."

"Are you sure?"

He nodded. "I've got to be up early tomorrow. And I have some work to do."

She smiled. "On the fireplace?"

"No. Just paperwork."

"All right, Mike. But I will see you soon?"

"Yes. Sure."

"Good. Because I have a surprise for you. I've taken a sublet over on East Fifty-eighth Street." One of her models was out of town on an assignment and had given Lucy free use of the place. Maintaining a hotel room on the chance that Mike would call her there was getting to be a ridiculous expense.

They rose at the same time. Lucy's arms slipped around his neck and she kissed him. Not a chaste kiss, either. Forgetting she was "Ellen" and not Lucy, she kissed him with passionate ardor.

Mike was stunned by the intensity of her kiss. It wasn't like Ellen at all. He resisted—for a moment. And then he was kissing her back.

Afterward, looking confused and disoriented, Mike cleared his throat. "I'll call you a cab."

Lucy tucked a key in his palm. "To my place. In case I'm in the shower or something when you drop by."

"MAYBE THIS WASN'T SUCH a good idea," Mike said anxiously.

Uncle Paulie gave his nephew a thorough study. "What do ya mean? Ya look like a million bucks, Trey."

Mike stared at his reflection in the full length mirror in his—that is, "Trey's"—borrowed SoHo loft. He was wearing black cowboy boots, black leather pants, a fuchsia undershirt that Uncle Paulie kept reminding him was La Ferlia's most popular color this year, and a hip-hugging black leather jacket.

To add a touch of "authenticity," Uncle Paulie splattered just a few dots of paint on the boots.

"Are you nuts? These boots cost over two hundred dollars. And they kill my feet. I'll probably end up with bunions."

"Quit squawking," Uncle Paulie said, checking out Mike's hairpiece. "Good. You're really getting the knack of it."

"I look ridiculous. I feel ridiculous."

"No good. I told ya, ya gotta drop your voice a couple of octaves. Try it again."

Mike smiled sardonically, but did as he was told. "I look ridiculous. I feel ridiculous. And now I sound ridiculous."

Uncle Paulie pursed his lips. "Too bad you can't add just a bit of a Polynesian lilt. Not to worry," he said hurriedly, seeing that Mike's frustration was starting to bubble over.

Mike moved to the window. "I think it's going to rain. I can't ride a motorcycle in the rain. It's dangerous."

Uncle Paulie joined his nephew at the large loft window. "There's not a cloud in the sky, Mikey. Hey, going to the gallery was your own idea."

"Pretending to be my rogue artist brother from Tahiti was yours."

Uncle Paulie gave Mike an affectionate squeeze. "You're gonna thank me one of these days, Trey, old boy."

"Trey," Mike muttered. "I can't believe I'm going to be introducing myself to my ex-wife as Trey."

"TREY. TREY AUSTIN Powell."

Lucy stared wide-eyed at the man in black leather. "You're kidding, right?" Her first thought, when she spotted him at the gallery, was that it was Mike in disguise, giving her a taste of her own medicine. And here she'd honestly thought Mike believed "Ellen" was for real.

"Kidding about what?" Mike asked ingenuously, meanwhile praying he wouldn't start to sweat too much, causing his makeup to streak.

Lucy gave him a closer scrutiny. Was it possible this wasn't her ex-husband? In her wildest dreams she couldn't imagine Mike going to this extreme to prove a point.

"You're telling me that my ex-husband is your brother?" Lucy asked warily.

"Yes. I imagine he's not one to brag about it," Mike said, watching her closely. He could see the shadows of suspicion and doubt playing on her lovely features. Was he really going to be able to pull this off?

"Brag? No, he certainly hasn't bragged," Lucy replied. "Actually, he never even mentioned you."

Mike gave her what he hoped was a roguish smile. "I didn't talk him up big in Tahiti, either."

Now Lucy's mouth dropped open. "Tahiti?"

"Gauguin was my idol as a kid."

Lucy eyed him skeptically. "Gauguin?"

"The artist who ran off to Tahiti . . ."

"Yes, I know who Gauguin was."

He smiled. "I thought you would."

"When did you return from . . . Tahiti?"

"A couple of weeks ago."

"Why?"

"Why?" Mike echoed. "Well, Tahiti's a great place to visit but I wouldn't want to live there . . . forever."

"Why not?"

Lucy wasn't making this easy for him. "Well, it's hot. Very hot."

"It hits ninety here in Manhattan in the summer," she challenged.

"But it isn't summer now. Anyway, I didn't just mean *hot* in that way," Mike said, dropping his voice another octave.

Lucy's whole expression changed. A rosy hue dotted her cheeks. "Oh."

Mike was amazed at himself for thinking so fast on his feet. And so in character. He concluded it must be something about the outfit, the whole make-over.

Lucy strolled over to a sculpture of two lovers embracing. Mike came up behind her. "I still can't believe you were married to my big brother."

She kept her back to him. "Why is that?"

He didn't answer.

"Have you seen . . . Mike?" she asked in a low voice.

"Briefly. We didn't have much in common when I left fifteen years ago and things haven't changed much." He hesitated. "I understand he's dating your sister now."

Lucy shut her eyes. "I guess. Ellen and I aren't . . . very close. We never were."

"From what my Uncle Paulie says, she's very different from you."

"Is that what Uncle Paulie says?" Lucy's throat was dry. "What else does he say? About Mike and . . . Ellen."

He stepped around the sculpture so that he was facing her. "I didn't pay much attention. I wasn't all that interested. I was more interested in you."

Lucy looked up sharply. She was convinced now that this man couldn't be Mike. Mike had charm, but it was innocent, boyish. He could never be so openly seductive. It wasn't in his nature. How ironic that she had fabricated a sister who was the exact opposite of her, when all the time Mike truly had a brother that was his real opposite.

"Uncle Paulie's very fond of you, Lucy," Mike said in his newly acquired baritone. "He talked a lot about you. I couldn't resist coming to see for myself."

"How did you know I'd be here?" she asked suspiciously.

Mike smiled to cover up for not having an answer to that question. He couldn't very well tell her Ellen had told him. Told Mike, that is. What would Cary Grant or Clark Gable have said?

"I must have a sixth sense about these things," he murmured, his gaze hooded.

She flushed.

Mike was again impressed with himself. Trey Austin Powell wasn't doing half badly.

"So, you're an artist," she said inanely.

"I've got a studio loft over in SoHo. Why not come back with me and decide for yourself?"

Lucy's cheeks positively blazed. Mike's brother was trying to seduce her. The nerve. The audacity. Why, if Mike knew— Would he care? He was busy being seduced by "Ellen." And as far as Lucy could tell, not minding the experience in the least.

Well, Lucy thought, giving Trey a fresh once-over, if "Ellen" was everything Mike wanted in a woman, wasn't Mike's wild, exotic, flamboyant kid brother everything she'd always thought she wanted?

"I've got my bike outside," Mike said, seeing the familiar indecision on her face.

"Bike? I'm afraid I haven't ridden on the handlebars of a bicycle for a long, long time, Trey."

He grinned. "Not that kind of a bike." He pointed out the window of the art gallery to the big, shiny Harley-Davidson parked out front.

Lucy stared in awe at the motorcycle. If she had any remaining doubts that this was Mike pulling her leg, those doubts instantly faded.

10

MIKE THANKED HIS LUCKY stars that he'd spent the last four days practicing riding his Harley, even going so far as to insist Uncle Paulie ride with him so he could get used to driving the monster with a passenger on board. He'd seen the reluctance in Uncle Paulie's face when he'd climbed on behind him, but after all, the bike had been his uncle's idea in the first place.

Although Mike felt confident about handling the bike now—even with a passenger—he hadn't anticipated the emotional effect on him of that passenger being Lucy. As she slid on behind him, her arms slipping around his waist, a current of desire shot through him. And never more than at this moment was he aware of the tight leather pants he wore.

"All set?" Mike asked as she snapped on the spare helmet.

"Let her rip," Lucy said with a tone of false gaiety.

As he zipped out into the traffic, Lucy's grip around his waist tightened. Mike's heart started to race faster than the engine. *Oh Lucy, Lucy, Lucy, how I've missed you!* Maybe Cary Grant or Clark Gable could have said it better, but neither of them could have meant it more.

"YOU'VE SETTLED IN pretty fast," Lucy said, standing nervously in the center of the large loft, most of which was used as a studio, with a small portion set aside as living space. There was no avoiding the very large mattress that filled a goodly portion of the living area. The bed wasn't even made—yet more proof that this man couldn't be Mike. Mike liked the bed to be made practically before he got out of it.

"I plan to fix the place up in time. Although I might decide to move to more upscale quarters. Maybe you could help me look for a suitable space. Something tells me our tastes would match quite nicely."

She deliberately turned from Trey and from that large unmade bed to focus on the canvases spread around the loft. These, like Trey's loft and Trey himself, were bold, larger than life, flashy, bordering on the extreme.

"So, what do you think?"

"There are . . . so many of them. You didn't do all these in two weeks."

He wore a blank expression.

"You said you've only been here for two weeks," she reminded him.

"Oh, right. I'd be a magician not an artist if I did all these in such a short time. No, I . . . shipped them over."

"All the way from Tahiti?"

"Yes. Wither I goest, goest my paintings."

She smiled. "That must have cost a fortune. Are you a successful painter, Trey?"

He stepped closer to her, unzipping his leather jacket.

Nervously, Lucy stepped back, nearly putting her heel through one of his canvases.

"I'm afraid I have a rather cavalier attitude toward money. And success. I like living for the moment, Lucy. When I see something I want, I don't sit around for hours, days, weeks, years, debating whether it's something I really need or I really can afford. I want it, I take it."

He was standing inches from her. He took off his jacket, feeling like an utter idiot in his fuchsia undershirt. Would Lucy really know it was a La Ferlia? Would she care? Was she attracted to him? Did she have the vaguest idea how aroused he felt? How much he wanted her?

"Not everything's ours for the taking, Trey," Lucy said carefully, eyeing first the outrageously expensive La Ferlia tank top and then the well-built body wearing it.

"No. I suppose not everything," he said huskily, his hand moving to her shoulder.

"What . . . are you doing?" Lucy asked breathlessly.

"Helping you off with your jacket. It's hot in here."

Lucy sidestepped him. *Hot* was the word, all right. Too hot for her to handle. "I really have to . . . go."

"But, baby, it's cold outside," Mike crooned.

Lucy thought Trey was a little over the edge.

"It's a song," Mike said with a rakish smile. "See, the guy keeps making up all these excuses for the gal to stay and she keeps making up reasons to leave. But, really she doesn't want to leave any more than he wants her to."

"I don't think I know that song," she muttered, starting for the door.

"Lucy?"

She stopped. "Yes?"

He came up behind her. "You never did tell me what you think?"

"What I think?" How could he expect her to think? She might never have another cogent thought again.

"About my paintings? Am I an artist?" And to himself, he thought, *I'm an artist, all right. A first-rate con artist!* Even while he was patting himself on the back for such a good opening performance, he felt like a heel. But it also felt so damn good to be wooing Lucy again. Only *he* wasn't wooing her. It was his fictitious brother, Trey, who was on the make. What had he gotten himself into?

"Yes. That is, you have a lot of talent. For art. Your work is . . . very colorful and exotic. Very . . . Tahitian."

"Women say 'sexy,'" Mike murmured against her ear.

Lucy certainly knew why. "I don't view art in that way," she said, stiffening as she felt his hand lightly brush the back of her neck.

"I wasn't talking about art."

"Really, Trey, you're . . . incorrigible."

"They say that, too."

"You're nothing like your brother."

"I'll take that as a compliment since you ditched my brother."

"I didn't . . . ditch him. You make it sound so callous."

"I just believe in telling it like it is."

"Mike's a terrific guy. It's just that the two of us . . ."

"Yes?"

Lucy felt it was wrong to discuss her former marriage to Mike with his brother.

"I really do have to go, Trey." She held up her hand. "Please, no songs."

He took her hand and pressed it to his lips. Her fingers were long and graceful. And cool to the touch. Or was it just that he was burning up?

When he let go of her hand, Lucy felt disoriented and then embarrassed. "You're a smooth operator, Trey."

"No, I'm not," he said with absolute Mike-like honesty. "You bring something out in me, Lucy, that no other woman ever has before."

Lucy emitted a disbelieving laugh. If only she knew how true a statement it was. The only lie was that "Trey" was saying the words, but Mike was the one feeling them.

She started for the door. "I can get a cab."

"Don't be silly," he said, slipping back into his black leather jacket. "I'll drive you home."

"On your bike?"

He winked at her. "On the handlebars, if you like."

"I'm not that daring," she confessed.

"How daring are you?"

Feelings tumbled over one another. Lucy couldn't sort out what was going on. There was no doubt she was attracted to Trey. He was sexy, gorgeous, said all the right things, made all the right moves. And she was feeling so confused, so vulnerable, so damn aroused. But was it Trey she wanted? Or his sweet, endearing, stuffy big brother?

Just as she started to turn away, impulse and desire made Mike pull her to him and kiss her. It had been so long since he'd kissed Lucy. He'd almost forgotten how delicious and soft her lips were. How inviting. Ellen's lips might have the same shape, but somehow kissing Ellen's lips felt worlds apart from kissing Lucy's. In that brief instant as he broke through Lucy's restraint and felt her respond in kind, he forgot that it was Trey kissing her. More to the point, he forgot that it was Trey Lucy was kissing.

He remembered soon enough. Reality crashed through as they broke apart. He was about to apologize to her, but then he realized that men like Trey—men who preached all that nonsense about seeing what they wanted and just taking it— wouldn't apologize for kissing a woman—even an ex-sister-in-law who was supposedly a veritable stranger.

"I'll take you home now," was what he said instead.

Lucy nodded weakly, mortified at herself for having kissed Trey the way she had. And here she'd been so angry at Mike for having come on to "Ellen" at their first encounter.

WHEN MIKE SHOWED UP in his Trey persona at the club, he was taken aback by the number of women giving him the eye. Uncle Paulie got a big kick out of it. He even introduced him around as his younger nephew, Trey. Even the regulars at the club didn't see through the disguise.

"So, how'd you do?" Uncle Paulie asked as he and Mike settled in a back booth away from the crowd and the music.

"You owe me five thousand bucks." Mike's voice reverberated with angst.

Paulie shrugged. "Hey, I'm the one that's gotta cough up the dough. I should have the long face."

"I never thought she'd...respond so enthusiastically," Mike muttered.

"So, she really went for your wild and crazy brother."

"She sure did. She certainly kissed him like she did."

"Kissed him?" Uncle Paulie was filled with newfound admiration for his nephew. "I knew you had it in ya, kid, but I didn't think you'd make such a fast move."

"I didn't think I would, either," Mike admitted. "It was just...being there with her again.... I don't know, Uncle Paulie. She looked so beautiful, so damn sexy. She was wearing this bright purple minidress and this whispery black silk jacket. Her hair was piled high on her head with these tendrils curling around her face. And her long legs. She was wearing these stockings that sparkled. She looked so good. So irresistible. I...I lost my head."

"Uh-uh, kid. Sounds to me more like you lost your heart."

Mike sighed. "What am I going to do? When I was with Lucy she seemed to fill every pore, every space in my body. Yet when I'm with her sister, Ellen—" He stopped, his mind in a complete muddle. "Ellen's such a nice woman, Uncle Paulie. She's—"

"I know. Sensible, practical, reasonable, blah, blah, blah." Uncle Paulie smiled crookedly.

"What's the matter with me? Why can't I figure out what I want?"

"There's nothing to figure out, Mikey. Look at yourself. Why do you think you went to all this trouble? Never mind. I'll tell ya. To win Lucy back, that's why. And when you were with Lucy tonight—when she was wrapped in your big, strong arms and the two of you were kissing passionately— did Ellen even enter your mind?"

"Not really," Mike confessed, feeling aroused at the memory of that kiss.

"Of course, she didn't. Because Ellen isn't Lucy."

Mike looked his uncle straight in the eye. "But I am Trey." He frowned. "Only I'm not Trey. Don't you see how confusing and out of hand this has all gotten?"

Mike rose, rubbing his forehead, only to find his tanning makeup coming off on his fingers. "I've got to go home and shower. And get out of these leather pants before my voice goes up two octaves instead of down two by the next time I see Lucy."

Paulie rose with Mike. "So, you've got a date lined up?"

"You mean, does 'Trey' have a date lined up?"

"Is it really all that tough having a split personality?"

Mike considered his uncle's question thoughtfully. "Not when I was with Lucy. I was actually on a roll. I was damn charming. It didn't feel that bad." He smiled wistfully. "Only, it didn't feel like me."

"YOU'RE STARTING TO SHOW," Lucy said when she met Stephie in front of Saks during her lunch hour the next day.

Stephie patted her slightly bulging tummy, her gaze fixed on her friend. "So are you."

"I'm not pregnant," Lucy gasped.

"That's not what I mean," Stephie answered wryly.

Lucy was amazed at Stephie's acuity, but she wasn't ready to get into the feelings that had kept her up half the night.

They walked into the swank department store. "Do you really want to shop?" Stephie asked, gently nudging Lucy as she examined a tray of perfumes at one of the counters.

"Of course, I want to shop. Shop Till I Drop. That's my motto," she said with false cheeriness.

Stephie followed her over to a table of scarves. Lucy idly fingered one, then another. Stephie plucked a fuchsia silk scarf from the pile. "You don't have one this color, do you?"

Lucy glanced over at the scarf. Suddenly, her eyes started to water.

"Let's get out of here," Lucy cried, bumping into a shopper as she spun around. "I'm . . . I'm sorry," she mumbled, rushing toward the exit.

Stephie gave the shopper an apologetic smile.

Lucy was waiting for Stephie outside on the street. Stephie took firm hold of her arm and steered her down the block. "Come on. Let's go splurge on totally fattening French food."

Lucy grimaced. "I . . . couldn't."

"Okay," Stephie said knowingly. "We'll do a liquid lunch. Milk shake for me and a bourbon on the rocks for you."

Lucy shook her head. "My stomach's tied in knots. Could we just go find a bench in the park?"

Stephie smiled sympathetically. "You are in a bad way when shopping, booze and gourmet food don't spark your spirits."

"My spark plugs are missing," Lucy said wanly. "And so's my mind."

"This sounds serious," Stephie said, waving for a cab to take them to Central Park.

"MAYBE THE CHILDREN'S ZOO wasn't such a smart idea," Stephie said as she watched Lucy eyeing all the squealing children, her expression a blend of envy and sorrow.

"Oh, no. It's nice here."

"Lucy, are you going to make me pull it out of you like a dentist?" Stephie asked wryly.

"I met Mike's brother yesterday."

Stephie burst out laughing.

"I know. I thought the same thing at first. But, it wasn't Mike. Believe me, it wasn't Mike."

"Lucy."

"All right, you can decide for yourself. I'm seeing him this evening. You can stop by at my place for cocktails before we go out to dinner. We're dining at Lutèce."

"Lutèce?" The restaurant was one of the poshest in town.

"Trey's choice, not mine. I'm learning to be moderate, remember?"

"Trey?"

"Trey Austin Powell. Mike's kid brother. Only he's no kid, believe me." Lucy proceeded to give her a thumbnail sketch of Mike's black-sheep brother.

Stephie laughed even harder.

"Would Mike ever have picked Lutèce?" Lucy argued. "It's one of the most expensive restaurants in the city. And Mike's stomach always acts up when he eats rich French foods. But Trey adores French cuisine. There's a big French influence in Tahiti."

Stephie laughed so hard, tears were running down her face. "Tahiti. I love it."

"It was really very romantic. He stowed away on a cargo boat when he was sixteen. He was very influenced by Gauguin...."

Stephie was clutching her stomach as she kept laughing. "Oh, Lucy. Stop."

"I was at his studio last night. In SoHo. I saw his paintings. There was a definite Gauguin flavor. And Mike can't even draw stick figures."

Stephie rummaged for a tissue in her large tote. "Oh, Lucy, don't you see what's going on? He's been on to you this whole time. And now he's seeing how you feel when the shoe's on the other foot."

"He has long hair and he drives a Harley."

Stephie stopped laughing. "A Harley? You mean a motorcycle?"

"A very large motorcycle."

"Mike?"

Lucy shook her head. "Not Mike, Stephie. That's what I've been trying to tell you. Trey."

Stephie had stopped laughing completely. She stared at Lucy, speechless.

"Cocktails tonight at my place? Seven."

Stephie nodded silently.

MIKE WAS SLIPPING ON his new Armani stretch jacket when his phone rang. It was Ellen.

"Hi. I just called to find out how your dinner meeting went last night." As "Ellen," Lucy had been making a concerted effort to show a sustained interest in Mike's work.

Mike had forgotten all about his supposed business dinner and it took him a few moments to respond. "Oh, right. Things went just fine."

"What's wrong with your voice? You sound a little hoarse. Poor boy. You aren't coming down with a cold, are you?" An opportunity for Lucy to show her maternal side.

It was no cold. It was just that Mike had been practicing "Trey's" voice for the past hour in preparation for his dinner date with Lucy. He cleared his throat. "Oh, no. Just a frog in my throat." He gave an uneasy little laugh.

"That's good. I know you hate being sick." Oops. "Ellen" didn't know that about Mike. Lucy did. "I mean, if you're anything like me. I hate being sick."

"Me, too," Mike said distractedly. If he didn't get Ellen off the phone he was going to be late picking up Lucy. "Listen, Ellen, I'd love to chat with you some more, but I've got—" He paused. He couldn't very well say, "I've got a hot date with your sister. Only don't be upset. It isn't really me who's dating her. It's my brother, Trey—"

"That's all right, Mike. Now it's my turn to have to sit through a dreary business dinner."

He prayed her meeting wasn't at Lutèce.

"Tomorrow evening, you're all mine, Mike. You're coming over to my flat and I'm going to cook you a marvelous English dinner. Roast beef and Yorkshire pudding. What do you say?"

What could he say without hurting her feelings? "That sounds wonderful, Ellen."

He hung up feeling like a complete heel.

CLARA PONDS AND EUNICE Blanford were stepping out of the Harkness Towers on their way to a symphony concert when they saw the large, noisy, black motorcycle pull up to the curb. Eunice nudged Clara.

"Why, look. It's Mike Powell."

With his helmet on, only his face visible, Mike did look more like himself.

Clara observed him, her expression clearly disapproving. She thought only hoodlums and gang members drove motorcycles. Never would she have imagined a man like Mike Powell on one of those devilish contraptions. But then, recalling those red silk panties of Lucy's discovered in his trouser pocket by the police, Clara concluded that the poor man really hadn't been himself since the divorce.

Eunice, who held a more romantic view of men on motorcycles, hurried over as he got off the bike. When Mike saw her approach he blanched. Luckily, his makeup kept his tan in place.

"Mike. It's so nice to . . ."

Before Eunice finished her greeting, Mike had removed his helmet and his long fake hair tumbled down almost to his shoulders.

Eunice blinked rapidly. "Oh, dear," she muttered.

Mike manufactured a blank stare.

Eunice glanced back at Clara. For a change, even Clara looked befuddled.

Mike took courage. "I'm afraid you're confusing me with my brother," he said in a deep, husky voice.

Eunice inspected him more closely. "Your brother is Mike Powell?"

Clara approached the pair, also giving Mike the once-over. "Mike Powell's brother, you say? I didn't know Mike Powell had a brother."

"Yes, Clara, but we also didn't know Lucy had a sister," Eunice reminded her companion.

Clara continued observing Mike closely. "We've never seen you before."

Mike smiled. Little did The Odd Couple realize they'd seen him just a short time ago and had tried to have him arrested.

"No," Eunice concurred. "We never have."

"I just moved here." Mike decided to omit the bit about having come from Tahiti. That required too much explanation and he knew the pair well enough that if he gave them the least opening, he'd be in for a session of twenty questions.

"Are you visiting Lucy?" Eunice asked.

"Or her sister, Ellen?" Clara inquired.

Mike felt weak-kneed. "Is Ellen up there with Lucy now?"

"Oh, so it's Lucy you've come to see," Clara surmised. Not that she was surprised. This rather wild-looking brother of Mike's didn't seem the prim, sedate Ellen Warner's type. Definitely more the type she could see coupled with Lucy. As she'd told Eunice many times over the months Mike and Lucy were married, she never could see those two as a successful matchup. Eunice, of course, constantly disagreed.

"Isn't that an extraordinary coincidence?" Eunice muttered as they watched Mike's "brother" enter the building. "Lucy having such a plain-looking sister and Mike having such a flamboyant brother." Her eyes strayed to the motorcycle, then returned to Clara. "You don't think Mike's brother and Lucy are . . . involved, do you?"

"In this day and age, Eunice, anything is possible."

MIKE FELT VERY UNEASY as he rang the doorbell to what had been, until recently, his own apartment. What if Ellen was there? Having to pretend to be Trey in front of both of them might be more than he could manage. Keeping up the pretense with Lucy wasn't going to be easy.

"IT'S SERENDIPITY, that's what it is," Jerry Benson was saying in Lucy's living room while Mike was gathering courage at the other side of Lucy's front door.

"Well, I'm from Missouri," Stephie quipped. "I've got to see it to believe it."

Lucy nervously glanced at the clock on the living room mantel. It was seven-fifteen. Trey was fifteen minutes late. Mike was never late. He was a stickler for promptness. It used to bother her, but now she realized there was no virtue in keeping people waiting.

"Maybe he changed his mind," Stephie commented. "Did you tell him we were joining you for cocktails? He might have decided he couldn't pull the wool over my eyes as easily as he had yours."

"I didn't tell him you'd be here. He's just . . . late." *Maybe he won't come at all*, Lucy thought with a mixture of relief and disappointment. After all, she was on this elaborate campaign to win back her husband. Why had she ever agreed to a date with Trey in the first place? But she knew why. Until Mike had come along, she had always been a sucker for men like Trey. Bad boys. Slick hipsters. Men with flash and socko sex appeal. Charmers. Men who were prone to brief affairs and short-lived romances. Trey was all those things. And something more. She saw some of Mike in him. Was that his real appeal?

Lucy jumped when the doorbell rang.

Jerry's eyes darted curiously toward the door.

Stephie, her mouth curled in an anticipatory smile, positioned herself for a good view of Trey as he entered the apartment.

Lucy's legs were wobbly as she crossed the living room in her three-inch spike heels, walking with funereal slowness. Looking at her, no one would ever have guessed she'd been a top model not so long ago and had gracefully walked miles of runways during her years in the business. She paused to collect herself as she got to the door.

WHEN THE DOOR OPENED and Mike stared into Lucy's large emerald-green eyes, he forgot all about his nervousness. Lucy's eyes seemed to him like sensual beacons, beckoning him. Her lips were painted a bright toffee color. What man in his right mind wouldn't want to taste such a delectable treat?

Tonight her outfit was even more provocative and alluring than the one she'd worn to the gallery opening—a gauzy honey-colored minidress, with a plunging V-neckline, cinched around her narrow waist with a cubist-print bright green and honey-colored satin sash. The green in the belt matched her eyes, the dress itself, her honey-gold hair.

"Hi," Lucy said, her voice a bare whisper as she took in Trey's trendy designer-cut spandex dinner jacket and matching trousers. Last night at the opening, he'd reminded her of James Dean in *Rebel Without a Cause*. Tonight, in that chic

Armani suit, with his deep golden tan, the modish long dark hair, the white silk scarf draped rakishly around his neck, he looked like a dashing, self-assured Hollywood leading man. But even though she felt definite vibrations as she stared at Trey, her mind once again strayed to Mike. He'd hated wearing evening clothes, always putting up a fuss when the occasion arose. Never in a million years would she have gotten her ex-husband into such stylish—not to mention expensive—fancy duds. It was Mike's feeling that a nicely tailored blue suit would do for almost all occasions. She used to tease him, saying that she believed he was the only baby in history ever born wearing a Brooks Brothers suit.

"You take my breath away, Lucy." Mike leaned toward her, picking up the familiar delicate whiff of her perfume. The scent was intoxicating, erotic.

A nervous smile grazed her lips. "Come in. I've invited a couple of others."

Mike froze: "Others?" *Oh, no,* he thought. *Ellen.*

"My best friend, Stephie Benson, and her husband, Jerry."

Not Ellen. Stephie. Stephie, Mike decided, was not a great improvement. The woman was as sharp as a tack. It was going to be no mean trick pulling one over on her.

"Trey?"

He was still standing at the open door.

He managed a smile that came off feeling, if not looking, pained and stepped inside the entry. Immediately he spotted Stephie, who was sitting in his favorite armchair that faced right out to the front door. She was staring at him like he was some rare find. Or like some not-so-rare fake!

Lucy slipped an arm through Trey's as she led him into the living room. She could feel his muscles quiver under the spandex material of the jacket. Was he nervous about meeting her friends or just glad to see her?

Stephie never took her eyes off him as Lucy made the introductions. Mike became increasingly convinced that she was going to pull his cover. He had horrible visions of her springing up from her—his—chair, tugging his hairpiece off with a vengeance, taking a tissue and rubbing it across his "healthy, glowing tan," and exposing him. The embarrassment and humiliation of that possibility nearly paralyzed him. It was way too soon to explain this idiotic hoax to Lucy. She'd be furious at him for such a low, underhanded stunt. He'd never get her back.

"Lucy tells me you've been living in Tahiti for years," Stephie commented idly as the hostess poured Mike a glass of wine and Jerry munched on a caviar-and-cracker appetizer.

Mike nodded. Forget Grant and Gable. He was going to try to play it like John Wayne—the strong, silent type.

"What's it like living in Tahiti?" Stephie prodded.

"Great." When a reply was required, he concluded it would be best to keep it monosyllabic if at all possible. But he could see that Stephie was just getting warmed up. He wasn't going to get away with a John Wayne approach for very long.

"I couldn't do it," Jerry piped in. "All those tropical diseases you'd have to worry about. Don't they have tsetse flies out there? Or killer bees?"

"Tsetse flies are in Africa. And killer bees are in South America," Lucy said, offering Trey a goblet of wine.

He took a large swallow. Stephie continued to observe him, her gaze shrewd. "Amazing how much you look like your brother," she remarked.

He smiled crookedly. "Lucy doesn't seem to think so."

Stephie glanced over at her friend. "Don't you, Lucy?"

"Well, actually, Trey, I said you were very different from Mike. Not so much in looks, though. Stephie's right, there. Your features and Mike's are quite similar."

Mike felt like he was sinking fast. Time to either bale out or come up with some way to plug the hole. And the only way to plug it was to behave in a way so unlike himself—that is, so unlike Mike—that even Stephie would have some second thoughts. Gathering up his courage and recalling all those films with suave romantic heroes Uncle Paulie had made him sit through, he sauntered over to Lucy and slipped an arm around her small waist.

"Even our lips?" he murmured in a voice deliberately loud enough for Stephie to hear.

He could tell from Stephie's expression that she was taken aback.

It was true. In her wildest dreams, Stephie could never imagine Mike behaving so provocatively. Although Lucy had always claimed he was a very amorous husband when they were alone, he had never been one to be demonstrative or seductive with Lucy when others were around.

Lucy was equally taken aback by Trey's suggestive remark. Her cheeks now a deeper hue than her rouge, she slipped away from Trey, avoiding Stephie's surprised look. As much as she'd always confided in her best friend, she had been too embarrassed and ashamed to confess that she and Trey had shared a passionate kiss in his studio last night.

Mike smiled rakishly at Lucy. "Sometimes it's the small differences that count."

Stephie broke into a laugh. Lucy's blush deepened. Jerry, busy spreading cheese on a cracker, didn't catch the joke. "What's so funny?"

Stephie slowly shook her head. "Never mind, dear. I think the joke's on me."

Lucy drank down her glass of wine and then nervously refilled it. On the one hand, she was glad Stephie was well on her way to being convinced Trey was legitimate. On the other hand, this little get-together was proving more of an ordeal than she'd expected.

She took a large swallow of her refill. "I was . . . telling Stephie what a . . . good painter you were, Trey."

"So, Lucy told you she came up to see my etchings last night," he quipped to Stephie after a sly glance at his ex-wife.

Lucy took another large swallow of her wine. Then another.

"Are you going to be showing in any galleries?" Stephie inquired, now almost as convinced as Lucy that Trey was the real thing. "Jerry and I are always in the market for artwork from hungry, young artists."

"I'm all three of those things," Mike said breezily. "A young artist, and hungry. But not for dough. I sell most of my stuff abroad. Actually, I'm just getting a shipment ready. But, if you'd like to drop down to my studio, Stephie, I might come up with something I'd be willing to part with for a reasonable price. And depending on how good you are at bargaining, you might even get my price down."

Stephie's mouth dropped open. So did Lucy's. Even Jerry, a bit dense about most things that didn't have to do with electronics, seemed a bit taken aback. *What an outrageous flirt!* Lucy thought with growing irritation.

Mike was getting carried away. He was so busy overplaying "Trey," he was oblivious to Lucy's annoyed reaction.

"And speaking about being hungry. . ." He paused, giving his ex-wife a newly practiced lean, hungry look. "We do have a dinner reservation, baby. And after dinner I'm going to take you to the 'rockingest' joint in town. We're gonna 'boogie on down,' sweetheart, until the wee hours of the morn." Mike had spent more money than he cared to think about on a crash dance course Uncle Paulie had insisted he take. Actually, after a disastrous start, he'd started to loosen up a little and get the hang of it. His instructor, a young woman with steel feet and the patience of Job, had told him he'd made miraculous progress—considering where he'd started from.

Stephie and Lucy shared astonished looks. If either of them had a single doubt remaining that Trey was real, they didn't now. Mike boogying on down? At a dance club? Not in a million years!

Jerry checked the time. "We need to get going anyway, Steph, if we want to catch a cab and make the eight o'clock movie."

"What are you going to see?" Mike asked.

"A new romantic comedy," Stephie said. "It's all about this woman who pretends she's married to this one guy and then her real ex-husband shows up and this other guy who her secretary hired to play her husband appears and she ends up juggling husbands all over the place while she tries to win a big deal with a German businessman who's anti-divorce."

Lucy blanched. She didn't know about coping with too many husbands, but she sure knew all about too many sisters. In this case, one was too many.

Mike was having much the same thought about brothers.

11

MIKE FLINCHED AS HE looked at the prices on the menu. And then there was the wine list. "Trey" would probably start with a pricey champagne, and then choose some positively extravagant wine for the main course. And the finest French cognac for after dinner. Not only was Mike bothered by the impact of the cost on his wallet, he was also worried about the impact of the rich food and alcohol on his stomach. Stowed away in his inside jacket pocket were several rolls of antacid.

A dignified waiter stood politely by. Mike gestured for him to come over.

"We'll start with a bottle of Dom Pérignon champagne. And why don't you have your wine steward select something to go with our dinners."

The waiter nodded.

"What would you like, Lucy?" Mike asked.

Lucy was already feeling the effects of the two glasses of wine she'd drunk in quick succession during the cocktail hour back at her place. She leaned a little closer to Trey. "I don't really think we need the champagne." Besides, she thought, it was ridiculously expensive and they were likely to leave more than half the bottle. It was a waste of money. She smiled to herself. "Ellen" really was beginning to rub off on her. Wouldn't Mike be proud of her newfound frugality?

"No one ever 'needs' champagne, silly goose." Mike then winked at the waiter, who responded with a discreet smile.

"I meant—" She stopped. What was the point of explaining? Men like Trey thrived on being extravagant. Maybe he was a successful artist, but Lucy doubted he had a penny in the bank. Any more than she'd had before meeting Mike. While she'd made a lot of money as a model, she'd blown most of it on frivolous indulgences—ski trips to Switzerland, surfing jaunts to Hawaii, designer clothes, a hardly-used beach house in Malibu, and endless other meaningless expenditures. Now, thanks entirely to Mike's sensible advice and guidance, she had a solid investment portfolio, plenty of money in the bank, even a hefty nest egg for her retirement. She'd teased him unmercifully about being a penny pincher, but she really was very grateful to him. And right now, she didn't see him as a tightwad at all. Just very wise and practical. Very unlike his spendthrift wastrel of a brother.

"Shall I order for us both?" Mike asked, stirring her from her reverie.

She tried to focus on her menu, but couldn't concentrate. She wasn't hungry. She didn't care what she ate. All of the offerings seemed so elaborate and so expensive.

"I'll have a salad. And an . . . iced tea."

Mike was baffled. What was this? Was she ill? Or did she think he couldn't pay the tab? Lucy loved eating in fancy restaurants and had never been shy about ordering whatever her heart desired—regardless of the cost. And this place was one she'd often hounded him to bring her to.

Lucy was annoyed when Trey ordered not only salads for them both, but Châteaubriand for two.

When the waiter left, Trey reached across the table and took hold of Lucy's hand. "I want to make you happy, Lucy."

"I would have been perfectly happy with a salad."

"I know we just met, Lucy. And I know that you were married to my brother. But something happened when I saw you last night. Something magical."

"Really, Trey..."

"He didn't appreciate you, Lucy. He couldn't have. If you were mine, I'd never let you go. And," he added, tightening his hold on her hand, "I'd never cramp your style. Because, oh, Lucy, you have such style."

He saw her chagrined expression and did wonder, then, if he was overplaying the part. The thing was, it wasn't all an act. He meant what he was saying—what "Trey" was saying. He regretted all those months of trying to change the irrepressible Lucy, hounding her to be more sensible, more practical, less frivolous. Lucy had such wonderful spirit, such panache. There was never a dull moment with her around. She made him laugh. She cheered him up when he got bogged down by pressures. She was the light of his life, the brightness, the glow. And Ellen? The truth was, poor Ellen was a nice, dull woman with no spark at all.

The waiter arrived with the Dom Pérignon. Arousal on Mike's part and nervous agitation on Lucy's made them both drink too much. The Châteaubriand and the wine that followed were probably divine, but all Mike could focus on was the lure of his ex-wife's presence; all Lucy could think about was how was she going to go "boogying on down" with this man after dinner was over? She was pretty sure that Trey didn't only have dancing on his mind. Not that he stood a chance of seducing her into bed.

For all his easy charm, Lucy was very wary of Trey. While he was certainly attractive and fit her usual "type" practically to the letter, she thought there was something superficial and insincere about him. As there was, she admitted now, about many of the suave types she'd dated in the past. Mike, who had depth and sincerity, had spoiled her forever for men like Trey.

She wondered how Mike felt about his brother. How he'd feel if he knew Trey was making a grand play for her. Would he be jealous? Or was he so caught up with "Ellen" that he'd merely wish his brother good luck, and good riddance to them both?

After dinner, Mike ordered a chocolate soufflé for them to share. He knew that Lucy adored anything made with chocolate. But when the steaming, aromatic delicacy arrived, all they could manage to do was pick at it.

When the bill came, Mike decided the best thing would be not to look at the total. Passing out at one of the poshest restaurants in town when presented with the tab would definitely not impress Lucy. With an insouciant gesture, he handed his credit card to the waiter, told him to take twenty percent for himself, and merely signed on the dotted line when the slip was returned, crumpling the customer copy into his jacket pocket. Later that night when he was alone and had a sparkling glass of bromo beside him, he'd uncrumple the sheet and face the music!

Before leaving the restaurant they both made quick trips to their respective rest rooms. Mike chomped down half a roll of antacids and Lucy took a tranquilizer.

THE DANCE CLUB WAS SMOKY, noisy, and crowded. The only reason Lucy had come was that this was the better of two choices, Trey's alternative suggestion having been to go straight back to his loft for some "slow dancing."

Mike guided her through the throngs to the dance floor. His head was woozy and the antacids hadn't entirely settled his stomach, but he was determined to show off his dance lessons to Lucy. Sure, there'd been that one magical night when he'd danced like a young Fred Astaire with her, but whenever Lucy had suggested they go dancing in public, Mike had always begged off. No more. Not only would he go dancing with Lucy in the future, he wouldn't have to worry about making an ass of himself on the dance floor.

Lucy had to admit that Trey was a good dancer. By the second dance, he had his jacket and tie off, his sleeves rolled up and his shirt unbuttoned practically to the navel.

As his confidence grew, Mike's dancing grew flashier and more outrageous. Still a little tipsy, the antacids having finally settled his stomach, he was really getting into it. A couple of times he even lost sight of Lucy. He became slowly aware of being watched by others on the dance floor. At some point they even formed a circle around him and Lucy, clapping to his moves. Mike felt a little like Patrick Swayze in the film, *Dirty Dancing*, another of his uncle's must-sees.

Lucy couldn't believe that Trey was so into the "beat" that he kept forgetting she was his partner. He was thoroughly enjoying putting on a public display for the other couples on the dance floor. Especially the young women. She thought Trey was a complete show-off.

Again, Lucy was struck by the sharp contrast between the two brothers. She thought about how much Mike hated being the center of attention. She'd always tried to cajole him into being more expressive, making more of a fashion statement, letting himself go a little. What if he'd followed her advice? He might have turned into a carbon copy of his exhibitionist brother. She should have counted her blessings. She'd give anything to have the opportunity to count them again.

"CLARA, DID YOU HEAR that?"

Clara rolled over in bed. "Go away, Eunice. I'm sleeping."

"It's after dawn, Clara. I was just out on the terrace looking for my reading glasses—would you believe they'd fallen into the potted geraniums?—and I heard something upstairs." There was a dramatic pause. "A commotion."

Clara's eyes opened. "A commotion? Upstairs?"

"And when I looked down into the street, do you know what I saw?"

"Please, Eunice. It's a bit early for twenty questions."

"That motorcycle," Eunice said in a conspiratorial whisper. "Do you know what that means?"

Clara sat up in bed. "Did you say it was six o'clock in the morning?"

"Six-fifteen," Eunice said with portent.

"Oh, dear," Clara murmured.

"Exactly."

Clara sat up in bed. Eunice had a bathrobe at the ready.

"What kind of a commotion?" Clara asked, slipping on the robe and stepping into her slippers. "China being thrown?"

"No. No china," Eunice replied, following Clara out of her bedroom. "Singing."

Clara stopped short. "Singing? You woke me up at the crack of dawn because you heard singing upstairs? Really, Eunice."

Eunice appeared aggrieved. "It was after the singing."

Clara was fully awake now. "After the singing?"

"She—Lucy—cried out."

Clara pursed her lips. "What kind of a cry?"

"She said, 'No tray. Please, no tray.'"

Clara blinked rapidly. "What kind of a tray? An ashtray? A serving tray?"

Eunice frowned. "Does it really matter what kind of a tray, Clara? What do you suppose he wanted to do with whatever kind of tray it was?"

"I can't imagine. What happened after Lucy cried out? Did he say anything?"

Eunice pressed her hand to her chest. "He said, 'Please say yes tray, Lucy.'"

"And?"

"And she said it again. 'No tray'."

They scampered across their living room to the open sliding door leading out to the terrace.

"And then?"

"And then there was silence. But just for a moment. And then she cried out, much sharper this time, close to hysteria if you ask me, 'No tray. I mean it. I can't do this.'"

Clara gripped the collar of her robe.

"Then there was silence again," Eunice continued in an agitated whisper. "This time it lasted for more than a minute. And then I heard her . . . sobbing."

They had stepped onto the terrace, both of them hearing her sob now.

Eunice gripped Clara's sleeve. "Do you think we should call the police?"

"PLEASE DON'T CRY, LUCY. I didn't mean to make you cry. It's just that I'm so crazy about you."

"You don't even know me, Trey," Lucy said, finally getting her tears under control. She didn't know why she'd gone so hysterical when all Trey had done was try to kiss her. She could have been more emphatic when she'd said no to him. It was all that champagne and food, all that dancing. She was exhausted, mentally and physically.

"I feel like I've known you for a lifetime," Mike said softly, equally wiped out, not to mention the painful bunions on his feet from having 'boogied' till nearly dawn. He fought back a yawn. Lucy was the night person, not him. He hadn't stayed up to see the sunrise like this since college.

Lucy dabbed at her eyes and stared at Trey. For just an instant there, his voice had sounded more like Mike's. Even his ardent expression reminded her of Mike. She smiled at him.

He smiled back. "You have a wonderful smile, Lucy." He reached out and lightly touched her cheek. "When can I see you again?"

Lucy pulled away from him. "I don't know, Trey. I don't—"

"Tonight." Oh, no. He couldn't see Lucy tonight. He was seeing Ellen. She was coming over to cook dinner for him. It wouldn't be right for him to cancel out at the last minute. "Wait . . ."

"I can't see you tonight, Trey." Tonight, she—that was, "Ellen"—was cooking dinner for Mike.

Mike was relieved Lucy couldn't make it, either. "Tomorrow night, then."

As she opened her mouth to protest, her doorbell rang several times in quick succession. Followed by pounding on her door.

Lucy and Mike shared puzzled looks. That was nothing compared to the expressions on their faces when she opened the door and they saw the anxious Odd Couple and the same two policemen that had almost thrown Mike into the clink a few weeks back.

Things weren't going well, but they quickly went from bad to worse when the older of the police officers gave Lucy the once-over and asked her if he was likely to find another pair of her silk panties in her "new boyfriend's" pocket.

Lucy was outraged. But Mike took it one step further. Maybe it was the result of being so much into his character of Trey. Or maybe it was pure frustration. Whatever the reason, mild-mannered Mike Powell punched the policeman in the jaw.

An hour later, Trey Austin Powell was sitting in a jail cell.

LUCY TRIED MIKE'S NUMBER again. Where could he be at seven o'clock on a Sunday morning? Had he been out with another woman last night? Had he stayed over at her place? Lucy felt her blood start to boil. Was he cheating on her? On "Ellen," that is?

She gave up and tried Uncle Paulie's number. After about the sixth ring a very disgruntled voice barked into the phone, "What is it?"

"Uncle Paulie, it's me. Lucy."

There was a moment's silence.

"Lucy? Is everything all right? Is Mike okay?"

"Mike? I really wouldn't know about Mike, Uncle Paulie," she said archly. "I wasn't calling about Mike. It's...Trey."

"Trey?" There was a blank note in Paulie's voice. It was very early in the morning.

"Your nephew. Mike's brother. He's . . . been arrested."

"Arrested? Mike?"

Lucy thought Uncle Paulie must be hung over. She wasn't getting through to him. "No, Uncle Paulie," she said very slowly, hoping her message would penetrate. "Not Mike. Trey. Trey's been arrested."

"Oh. Oh, Trey. My nephew, Trey." Paulie's wits were starting to return.

"Yes. Actually I phoned Mike first, thinking he might want to go down to the station house and see about bailing Trey out. But he wasn't home."

"Oh. Really?"

"Really."

"What exactly was Trey arrested for, Lucy? It didn't have anything to do with that motorcycle, did it?" Mike would never forgive him for talking him into renting that contraption.

Lucy placed an ice pack on her head. "No, Uncle Paulie. It had nothing to do with his motorcycle. Although, I don't particularly think riding around Manhattan on a bike is really all that smart. Especially the way he rides it. He's reckless."

"Lucy, why was Trey arrested?"

Lucy sighed. "It was all The Odd Couple's fault." She paused. "No, it was my fault, really. I shouldn't have let Trey come back up to my apartment in the first place. But he wasn't all that steady on his feet. And he said all he wanted was a cup of black coffee. But that wasn't all he wanted. Not that he...overstepped his bounds. Well, he tried to. Not that he tried anything really...untoward. I started to cry. And once I got started, I couldn't seem to stop. And I suppose that's what got The Odd Couple downstairs worried again. That, and they mistook 'Trey' for 'tray.' They thought he was trying to do something indecent to me with a tray and I was resisting. When the police asked them what they imagined he might do to me with a tray, they couldn't actually give them an answer."

"Lucy," Uncle Paulie broke in finally when she stopped to take a breath. "Do me a favor and cut to the chase."

"The chase? Oh, there was no chase."

"I mean," he said with exaggerated patience, "why did the cops arrest Mi—Trey."

Lucy readjusted the ice pack. "You see, when the police showed up at my door, it turned out to be the same two cops who'd come up to my apartment a few weeks back. The ones who thought Mike was...well, that he'd murdered me. And now The Odd Couple had told them I was being assaulted by Mike's brother. So anyway, the police were about to leave once they saw that I was fine, but then before they turned to go, one of them made an insulting reference to my...panties, and—"

"Lucy, are you sober?"

"No," she admitted wanly. "Not entirely."

"Okay, go on," he coaxed gently. "There was this reference to your...panties."

"Yes. And so Trey hit him in the jaw."

"*Trey* punched out a cop?"

"Well, he didn't really hit him all that hard. He was still pretty unsteady on his feet. But he did assault an officer." She set down the ice pack and rubbed her head. "I would have gone down to bail him out myself, but it's Sunday and I don't have enough cash on hand. So, I called Mike. But then he wasn't home." She hesitated. "You don't . . . happen to know . . . where he might be?"

Uncle Paulie bit back a chuckle. "I think I have a good idea."

"Oh," Lucy said, her voice laden with disappointment.

"He's not with a dame, if that's what you're thinking, Lucy."

"I wasn't thinking . . ." she lied.

"I can guarantee you that. And as for Trey, you just leave everything to me. I have a pal who's a police chief who can probably pull a few strings. I'll have Trey out of the can within the hour."

"Thanks, Uncle Paulie."

"So, Lucy, you like him?"

"Trey?"

"That was pretty gallant of the kid to punch out a cop for your honor. You think Mike would ever have done that?"

Lucy had to smile. "I can't exactly picture it," she admitted.

"Yeah. Trey's something, all right."

Lucy couldn't argue with Uncle Paulie's summation.

UNCLE PAULIE WAS TRUE to his word. By nine-fifteen that morning, he dropped his nephew off at his apartment. Mike reached for the door handle.

"Listen, kid—"

"Don't say a word, Uncle Paulie. Just don't say anything."

A wan smile on his face, Uncle Paulie nodded.

HE WAS COMING OUT OF the shower when he heard his down-stairs buzzer. Wrapping a towel around his waist, he left wet footprints as he padded down the hallway.

"Mike?"

His breath caught. "Lucy?" Her name came out in a gasp.

"Can I come up?"

"Up . . . here? Oh, well, sure. Sure, Lucy. Come on up." After buzzing her in, he raced back to the bathroom only to slip on the wet hallway floor just outside the bathroom door. His feet went out from under him and he went crashing to the floor, landing with a heavy thud. With the wind temporarily knocked out of him, he lay there unable to breathe. When he finally managed to get up, the doorbell was ringing. Securing the towel he had draped around his waist, he went back down the hall to let Lucy in.

She wasn't expecting to see him dressed in a bath towel.

"Lucy." His voice was raspy, a combination of having been up all night, then trapped for several hours this morning in a jail cell where every other inmate smoked, and finally nearly knocking himself unconscious. And then there was Lucy's surprise arrival.

"Are you . . . alone?" she asked hesitantly.

"Alone?" Only then did he realize his state of dress, or undress, as it were. Did Lucy suspect that Ellen was there? "Yes, Lucy. I'm alone."

"I just thought, maybe . . . Trey was here."

"Trey? Here? Oh, no. No. This is the last place Trey would be," Mike said emphatically.

Lucy frowned. "He wasn't at his loft. And I knew Uncle Paulie had sprung him." She paused. "Did you know he was in jail?"

"Uh . . . yeah. Uncle Paulie gave me a call."

"Did he give you the . . . details?"

Mike shrugged, turning away from Lucy. "I should go put something on."

"That's okay."

Mike did a double take.

Lucy flushed. "I mean, I should be leaving. I was just looking for . . . Trey. I wanted to make sure he was okay."

So, she'd come looking for him. She was concerned about him. That had to mean she cared about him. It was funny, but he felt good and bad about it at the same time. It was almost as if she had fallen in love with another man. He had to keep reminding himself he *was* that other man.

"You two must have hit it off," he said offhandedly.

Lucy swallowed hard. "He's . . . really something," she muttered, echoing Uncle Paulie's earlier assessment.

Mike nodded. "Yeah. My brother Trey's a wild and crazy guy."

"I should get back home. Maybe he went over there."

"I suppose . . . it's possible."

"You're wet."

"I was in the shower."

"Sorry for disturbing you."

"Oh, you weren't disturbing me, Lucy." *Liar.* She caused a flurry of disturbing sensations. "I was . . . finished. Showering."

"I hear you and . . . Ellen have a dinner date tonight." She couldn't quite look him in the eye. "You two have hit it off, too, it seems."

"Well . . ." Mike wished he could tell Lucy the truth—the truth about his feelings for Ellen, at least. But he was still worried that she might feel he'd taken unfair advantage of her sister.

"Ellen can't say enough good things about you," Lucy said, trying to keep her gaze off Mike's broad bare chest.

"Really?"

"Really. She says you're so clever and discerning."

Mike's eyes widened. "Discerning?"

"Astute, intelligent, reasonable . . ."

"I think she's gotten a little . . . carried away," Mike muttered, embarrassed.

"Oh, no. I told her she was absolutely right. She has your number, Mike."

He stepped closer to her. "You think so?"

His gaze caught hers and held her captive. The gentle timbre of his voice sent strange vibrations coursing through her. He looked so good, standing there, naked save for a skimpy white bath towel. And he smelled so good—all fresh and soapy.

Mike was equally entranced by Lucy. When he was with Ellen, he was reminded even more of his longing for Lucy. If only he could just come right out and tell her he wouldn't want to change a single thing about her; that he loved and adored her just the way she was . . .

Lucy stepped back. It wasn't an easy move, but she kept thinking, *Wait until tonight*. Tonight, when "Ellen" cooked him dinner over at her place, Lucy would pursue Mike with undaunted energy. Once Mike committed himself physically and emotionally to the "new" her, she'd tell him the truth and explain that she only wanted to prove to him that she could be the kind of wife he wanted. And also prove to him that she truly did love him just the way he was. Then she would break it gently to Trey. . . .

"I'll see you, Mike," Lucy mumbled, her hand gripping the door knob.

"When?" Mike asked without thinking.

Lucy almost said, *Later tonight*. "I don't know."

Mike nodded. He had to fight to keep from smiling. Little did she know that she'd be seeing him tomorrow evening. He had it all planned—the grand seduction scene over at his studio in SoHo. He would win her over, make passionate love to her, and confess the truth, telling her that he'd only carried out the masquerade to prove he could be the kind of man she wanted. Then he would break it gently to Ellen....

12

"LUCY, ARE YOU SURE YOU know what you're doing?" Stephie asked as Lucy pored over a cookbook in the kitchen of her borrowed studio apartment where she'd spent the night "to get more into character." Still in her bathrobe, she'd been agonizing all morning about the "perfect" meal to make for Mike. Finally, she'd cajoled Stephie into coming over to give her some advice and lend her a little moral support.

"If I knew what I was doing, I wouldn't be here asking for your help," Lucy countered as she turned a page with nervous agitation. "What do you think of pheasant under glass, wild rice and truffles, fresh asparagus?"

"I'm not talking about the cooking. I'm talking about this whole crazy charade."

"It isn't a charade. Not in the real sense of the word. I may be pretending to be my sister, but my feelings are all mine. I have truly come to appreciate Mike for who he is. And, being "Ellen," I've learned to be more . . . discerning and . . . astute. And frugal."

Stephie grinned. "Pheasant under glass? Wild rice? Truffles?"

Lucy frowned. "Okay, so I'm still learning. I'll go back to the roast beef and Yorkshire pudding. It's just that when I tried making the Yorkshire pudding at home the other night, it tasted more like school paste. Not that I've actually ever tasted school paste, but . . ."

"Lucy, what about just ordering in a pizza and coming clean?"

Lucy shut the cookbook. "I *am* going to come clean. After I'm sure that Mike really does feel about me—about "Ellen"—the way I think he does."

"Did you ever consider that he might be fit to be tied when you drop the truth on him? I have a feeling he thinks you and his brother are . . ."

"We aren't," Lucy said emphatically. "And we won't. I couldn't. He . . . wouldn't. Well, he would if he could, but he can't. It's as simple as that."

Stephie rolled her eyes. "Forget it. Come on. I'll teach you how to make Yorkshire pudding."

Lucy gave her friend a bear hug. "You'll see, Steph. It's all going to work out." She released Stephie and dug into a shopping bag resting beside the kitchen table.

Stephie laughed when Lucy pulled out her new purchase. It was a frilly white apron. Emblazoned in red across the front were the words, We're Cooking Now!

"YOU'VE REALLY THOUGHT of everything, Ellen," Mike said as he watched her set ivory candles in cut-glass holders, both of which she'd purchased along with her apron. She hadn't shown him the apron yet. She was saving that. The pièce de résistance!

"I hope so, love," Lucy said in a throaty British accent. "I really want this to be a very special night." She crossed the room and slipped a disc into the CD player. Harry Connick, Jr., began singing Gershwin. She turned back to Mike and smiled coquettishly.

Mike smiled back, but it was a nervous smile. There was something different about Ellen tonight. She seemed like a woman with a mission. And he had a pretty good idea what that mission was. Or rather—who!

"The roast beef smells great." *That's it,* Mike told himself. *Keep the focus on food.* "I haven't had a good home-cooked meal in ages."

Ellen laughed dryly. "I doubt you got many of them when you were married to Lucy. How often did she make you a nice home-cooked meal?"

Mike bristled. "Lucy worked all day. She didn't have any more time than I did to whip up a big home-cooked meal."

"What about on weekends?" she persisted.

"We were . . . always on the go. Engagements, parties, functions, trips."

"Poor love. She ran you ragged. And I bet all you wanted to do most of the time was relax on the weekend, watch a ball game, maybe visit with a few close friends. Well, that's over and done with."

"Yes," Mike said quietly. "That's over and done with." Unless he could do something about it tomorrow evening.

Lucy sauntered over to him and put her arms around his neck. "I hope you're going to like my Yorkshire pudding, love."

"Oh, I'm . . . sure I will," Mike mumbled. "Shouldn't I light the candles?" he suggested as he extricated himself from her embrace.

"Yes, love. You do that and then make yourself comfortable. Have a look around if you like. I'll go check on the meat."

While Lucy was in the kitchen, Mike sat on a chair in her small, spare living room weighing the pros and cons of coming clean with Ellen. He bemoaned ever having gotten himself into this mess. And now that he was in it—up to his neck—he didn't know how to get out of it without hurting Ellen and angering Lucy. He decided that all he had to do was get through this dinner, after which he would tell Ellen he wasn't feeling well. A headache. No, that was too trite. The flu. Not much better. And she'd probably want to take him home herself and nurse him.

He knew. A business engagement. Some kind of emergency, completely unexpected. Hurrying over to the phone, he called his uncle at the club. "Don't worry, kid. I won't forget. You want me to phone Ellen's place in one hour and tell you—"

"You don't really have to tell me anything," Mike said hurriedly, nervous that Ellen would come popping out of the kitchen.

"Isn't she gonna think it's odd, a business associate calling you at her apartment? Won't she ask how he knew where to reach you?"

"Don't worry. I'll tell her I left the number because of this important business deal— She's coming. Don't forget. One hour." Mike figured that would give them time to eat dinner and not enough time for dessert!

"Here we are," Lucy said, proudly carrying out a tray of roast beef, Yorkshire pudding, and other trimmings.

While they ate Mike kept up a steady banter, praising the food—which really was quite delicious—and mentioning several times that he was right in the middle of a big business deal and even had to leave his number wherever he went. Now that he knew he was going to get reprieved before things got out of hand, he was very bright and effusive.

Lucy was thrilled. Mike was in a terrific frame of mind. She gave him second helpings of dinner and told him how much fun it was, cooking for a man who appreciated her talents so much.

It was just about an hour when they finished eating and Lucy started clearing away the plates. "Wait until you see what I've got for dessert," she said gaily.

As she left the room, Mike anxiously checked his watch, then glanced over at the telephone as if his gaze could will it to ring. What if Uncle Paulie had forgotten? *No,* Mike reassured himself. *He probably just got tied up with a customer for a few minutes.* There was still time. Dinner wasn't over yet. Or so he thought.

"Oh, Mike. Mike, love. Would you mind bringing in the dessert plates?" Lucy called from the kitchen.

Mike gathered up the two small plates, one in each hand. He hoped that Ellen had made a big dessert even though he was stuffed. He was bound and determined to keep on eating until the damn phone rang.

With one ear listening for that ring, Mike blithely stepped into the kitchen, dessert plates in hand. They slipped out of his grip and crashed to the floor as he stared openmouthed at Ellen. She was wearing a frilly white apron. That was all she was wearing!

"Dessert's on," Lucy said with a coy smile.

Mike was speechless.

And then the phone rang.

"I DON'T WANT TO TALK about it," Mike muttered a short while later as Paulie set a Scotch on the rocks in front of him, back at the club.

"Did I ask you anything?"

"No, but you want to ask."

"Not me, Mikey. Curiosity killed the cat."

Mike took a sip of the Scotch and then shivered. "She was wearing this apron."

Paulie bit back a smile. He knew his nephew like the back of his hand. "Lots of women wear aprons," he said blandly.

There was a pregnant pause. "That's all she was wearing."

Uncle Paulie's eyes widened. "Ellen?"

Mike nodded solemnly. "Ellen."

"I can't picture it. Ellen?"

"Ellen."

"Well, well, well."

Mike scowled. "Things certainly got more out of hand than I ever dreamed." He finished off his drink. "I'll tell you one thing, though. Getting involved with Ellen has totally convinced me just how much I love Lucy."

"I doubt that's going to be any consolation for Ellen, Mikey."

"Tell me something I don't know."

STEPHIE EDGED AROUND the broken plates that Mike had dropped on the kitchen floor and then sidestepped the apple pie that Lucy had flung off the table after Mike's hasty departure. She got to the sink and poured Lucy a glass of water.

"Here. Drink this."

Lucy was sitting at the kitchen table, her raincoat thrown over her apron, her head cradled in her arms. "I am so humiliated."

"But you told me on the phone he had to leave because of a business emergency," Stephie soothed.

"You didn't see the look of relief on his face when he got that call. Or the skid marks he left when he raced out of here. My brilliant plan didn't work. I did everything right. It was going so well. At least, I thought it was going so well. My Yorkshire pudding was . . . perfect." Lucy started sobbing quietly again.

"The apple pie looks pretty good, too," Stephie teased affectionately.

Lucy raised her head. Her eyes were all red. "I did my best. I made myself into exactly the kind of woman that he always wanted me to be. So, what went wrong?"

"Sometimes, Luce, what we think we want isn't what we want at all."

Fresh tears ran down her cheeks. "I know. I know."

MIKE WAS A NERVOUS WRECK. Lucy had left a message on his answering machine at his borrowed artist's studio that she would meet him there tonight. After their last encounter when just a kiss had brought out the police, he'd worried that she wouldn't trust him to be alone with her again. Now he was worried that she wasn't worried.

"Will you relax?" Uncle Paulie pleaded. "You're gonna wear out the carpet."

"I'll buy him a new carpet," Mike said distractedly.

"See what I mean. There *is* no carpet."

"What?" Mike looked down. "Oh."

Paulie grinned. "This is what you wanted, isn't it? For Lucy to fall for the new you?"

"But she doesn't know it's the new me. She doesn't know it's *any* me. She's fallen for my brother. She's about to be seduced by another man."

"Mikey, Mikey. You're nuts, you know that. You're the other man."

"But she doesn't know that. It's as if she's being unfaithful to me . . . right before my eyes."

Paulie's grin broadened. "Hey, hotshot. She hasn't fallen under your macho-hunk spell yet. Don't count your chickens."

"Why did she decide to meet me here, then? I could tell by the tone of her voice on the answering machine that she was . . . ready to take the plunge."

"I've heard of mind readers and palm readers," Uncle Paulie quipped, "but voice readers?"

Mike threw up his hands. "I'm being crazy."

"Now we're talking sense," Paulie said, chuckling.

"I mean, this is exactly what I wanted. This was the plan. And it's working. I'm about to prove to my ex-wife that I can be the man she always wanted. What am I worrying about?

It's great that she wants me, even if it isn't me. Because it *is* me, right?"

Paulie grabbed his jacket and started for the door. "If I stay here any longer, kid, they're gonna be carting us both off to the funny farm."

"Hey," Mike called out as his uncle started out the door. "Aren't you going to wish me luck?"

Paulie glanced back. "I wish you both luck."

"Me and Lucy?"

Paulie winked. "No. You and 'Trey'."

LUCY HELD UP A CLINGY, scoop-necked, turquoise jersey dress that left little to the imagination. "What do you think?" she asked, holding it in front of herself in the full-length mirror.

"Are you sure you know what you're doing, Lucy?"

Lucy turned from her mirror to her bed where Stephie and her two-year-old, Amy, were playing with wooden blocks. Stephie would get a few blocks stacked on top of one another and then Amy would jump on the bed, knocking them over. This caused the toddler no end of amusement.

Lucy's eyes zeroed in on Amy. "I'm sure," she said with a wistful expression. It was almost as if she could actually hear her biological clock ticking.

"It's not Trey you want, Lucy. It's his brother. I just hope you come back to your senses before you do something really dumb."

"What was dumb was trying to think I could make myself into someone else. Trey adores me just the way I am. He thinks Mike was nuts for not appreciating my special qualities." She slipped off her cotton bathrobe, revealing a very sexy white lace teddy. "Trey and I are . . . simpatico. He's incredibly sexy, a fabulous dancer, and he doesn't sit around counting his pennies."

"That's because he spends them too fast," Stephie commented dryly, attempting to put a fourth block on the stack before Amy bounced.

Lucy slipped the dress over her head. It fit like a second skin. Stephie gave a wolf whistle, but it held a sardonic note.

"I like Trey. I find him very attractive and appealing," Lucy said with meager enthusiasm.

"Right. That's why you burst into tears when he tried to kiss you."

"It wasn't the kiss. It was what I figured was going to follow the kiss. I just wasn't . . . prepared."

"And now you're prepared?" Stephie asked skeptically.

"Yes."

"Right. Sure, Luce. Last night you try to seduce your ex-husband whom you have gone to incredible lengths to win back. And tonight you're prepared to be seduced by his irresponsible, incorrigible brother."

Lucy scowled. "I made a mistake. I should never have—"

"No. You haven't made a mistake, Lucy," Stephie said, cutting her off. "But you're about to."

"You haven't given Trey a chance, Steph," Lucy argued as she tended to her makeup.

"I'm sorry, Lucy, but Trey's the kind of guy if you give him an inch he'll grab . . . well, more than I'd want grabbed."

Lucy's cheeks reddened and she hadn't put her rouge on yet. "Being flirtatious is just part of his style. He doesn't mean anything by it. I think underneath all that macho come-on is a very sweet, endearing man."

Stephie laughed dryly. "You've got a very vivid imagination," she said, scooping up her giggling daughter and rising from the bed.

"I really do know what I'm doing, Steph."

Stephie smiled wryly. "Well, if you discover you don't, maybe this time the SWAT team will show up to rescue you.

Then again, over at Trey's studio you won't have The Odd Couple eavesdropping and looking out for your welfare."

MIKE READ THE instructions on the self-tanning cream he was about to apply. He couldn't risk make-up to create his tan tonight because it was likely to rub off when he and Lucy. . .

Just the thought of once again making love to Lucy pushed all his worries from his mind. He smiled cockily at his reflection in the mirror. "Tonight's the night, Mikey." And then he reminded himself that he was "Trey" until after the grand seduction.

LUCY STEPPED OUT OF THE cab and nervously regarded the converted warehouse. Up there on the eighth floor, Trey was waiting for her in his artist's loft. This time it wasn't his etchings she'd come to see. After last night's disaster with Mike, she had managed to almost convince herself that Trey was the right man for her, after all.

Now that she'd arrived, she couldn't quite muster up the same confidence she'd had earlier, thanks in no small part to Stephie. Sometimes, Lucy decided, Stephie was too smart for her own good. And for her *good*, as well.

She hesitated as she got to the outside door, her finger poised but not pressing the button to Trey's studio. Was she doing the right thing? Was she settling for second best? Was this her way of drowning her sorrows over Mike's rejection of "Ellen"? It was pretty awful feeling a dual rejection, first as herself, then as her sister.

Resolutely, she pushed Mike from her mind and pressed the buzzer. Mike jumped when the buzzer went off. An attack of nerves assaulted him and all his worries returned—along with a surfer-size wave of guilt. Should he come clean right from the start? But chances were, if he did, Lucy would turn on her heel and storm out before he got the chance to explain everything—his motives, his feelings, his desperation to win her back.

It would be different, once they'd made love. She'd be in a more receptive frame of mind. She'd also hopefully be naked and in his arms, so fleeing wouldn't be quite so easy.

He pressed his buzzer to let her in.

UPON SEEING LUCY wrapped in clinging bright turquoise, Mike was left so flustered and breathless he forgot all the lessons in "suave" he had learned over the past weeks.

"Lucy. It's . . . you. I mean . . . you're here."

Lucy was too nervous to notice Mike's incoherent babble. He tried to pull himself together. "Come on in."

Lucy hung back at the door, idly looking around the studio.

"Lucy?"

She stepped inside. Not a lively step.

Mike was too nervous to notice. He grabbed up the two wineglasses he'd filled after buzzing Lucy in, handing her one, watching her take her first sip. Her second. Her third. She stopped after the fourth sip, aware of his eyes on her.

He took the glass from her hand, set it down on a shelf along with his untouched wine and drew her into his arms.

"Trey . . ."

He smiled. "You aren't going to start crying again, are you, Lucy?"

"I'm not sure," she admitted.

He continued holding her. Lucy relaxed a little, her body curving into his. He was built so much like Mike—*No, no,* she chided herself. She mustn't think about Mike. She had to stop making comparisons. It wasn't fair to his brother. Trey was his own person.

As he felt her resistance give way, Mike's heart lurched, longing blanketing all his guilt and worries. "Oh, Lucy," he murmured, releasing her but taking hold of her hand. He pressed it to his lips. Then he switched off the light and led her across the studio to his "living space."

That big double bed lit by a bedside lamp loomed before Lucy like Satan's lure. She was going to hell, pure and simple, with Trey leading the way. And she wasn't even doing anything to stop him.

When they got to the edge of the bed, Mike took her in his arms again. He hesitated for a moment before kissing her. Her eyes were closed, her head was tilted invitingly, or at least willingly. Softly, lovingly, he pressed his lips to hers, taking his time, savoring the sensations, the sheer joy of the experience.

Lucy squeezed her eyes shut. Oh, God, he was even kissing her like Mike, now. Why didn't he just devour her, ravage her mouth, be rough and macho? Why didn't he kiss her like she expected a man like Trey to kiss her? She'd told herself the only reason she was here tonight was because Trey was the antithesis of Mike. Leave it to the bastard to go and prove her wrong. Was everyone against her?

He loosened the clip that kept her hair piled high. It cascaded down around her shoulders. He slipped his fingers through the strands, his strokes tender and delicate.

Was he trying to drive her crazy?

His lips traced a line from her forehead to her chin, then down her throat.

Lucy just stood there, rooted to the spot, confusion and arousal swirling around her.

Mike's hands found their way to the zipper of her dress. The zipper glided down effortlessly.

She kept her eyes closed but she could hear the rustle of clothes—his, now.

"Open your eyes, Lucy." His voice was huskier than before.

She was slow to follow his command.

"Do you know how special you are to me?" he murmured. He was bare-chested and the snap of his jeans was undone, the zipper down just an inch so that he looked like a sexy magazine ad.

Lucy's gaze trailed over his body. Except that he was so much tanner than Mike, they could have been twins. She shut her eyes again for an instant to eradicate the thought.

When she opened them again, she looked directly into Trey's eyes. Even his eyes were so much like Mike's. *Damn, damn, damn.*

"I'm . . . fond of you, too, Trey," she mumbled, more to break the silent tension that only she seemed to be experiencing.

"Are you, Lucy?" he prodded, slowly edging her dress off her shoulders, punctuating the move with soft, moist kisses on her creamy skin.

"Yes. But . . ."

"But what?" he whispered, the dress slipping to her waist, her hips, puddling down around her ankles on the floor.

She felt as good as naked standing there in her lacy white teddy. And not nearly as good as she told herself she should be feeling.

"Trey?"

"Yes, Lucy?" He tugged her gently down onto the bed with him. Then he leaned over her to light a candle and turn off the lamp. Instead of rolling back beside her, he hovered over her, braking his weight with his hands.

"Maybe we're . . . moving too fast, Trey."

Almost in slow motion, he kissed one corner of her mouth, then the other. "Is that too fast?"

"It's just that I'm . . . not sure how I . . . feel," Lucy protested, albeit weakly. There was something different about Trey tonight. Gone was that cocky, 'I take what I want' kind of attitude and approach. He was being so sweet, so tender, so enticing. She wasn't prepared. . . .

"You feel wonderful, trust me," he murmured, his hand gliding up her arm and then delicately lowering first the right strap, then the left strap of her teddy.

Her hands lurched to his wrists, stopping him from lowering the teddy down over her breasts. "Wait, Trey."

He wanted her so much, he'd waited so long. Too long.

"I . . . I can't do this," she cried, her voice breaking into a sob.

Mike was utterly perplexed as he watched the tears spill from her eyes. "Lucy, talk to me. Tell me what's the matter. Is it something I'm doing wrong?"

She shook her head, the tears coming full force now. She pushed him roughly from her and leaped from the bed. "It isn't you . . . Trey. It's me. It's Mike. It's . . . It's everything."

She fled into the bathroom, slamming the door behind her and turning the lock.

13

MIKE RAPPED LIGHTLY on the bathroom door. "Lucy, Lucy, don't cry. It's okay. Whatever you want is okay. Maybe we were moving too fast. We can go slower. I mean, really slower. Please come out and we'll talk. Honest, Lucy. Just talk."

There was no response. He pressed his ear to the door to find out whether she was still crying. He couldn't hear a thing. Panic began to suffuse him. She wouldn't have gone and done something crazy...?

LUCY HAD FELT NAKED standing in the bathroom in her teddy so she'd grabbed Trey's robe, which was hanging on a hook on the door. After slipping it on, the tears still flowing, she'd caught a glimpse of her image in the bathroom mirror. For several long minutes, all Lucy could do was stare dumbly at her reflection, her gaze riveted not on her tear-streaked face, but on the rolled collar of Trey Austin Powell's robe. His monogrammed robe. Only it was the wrong monogram. M.L.P. Michael Lloyd Powell. It was the very robe she'd given her ex for his birthday.

What the hell was it doing hanging on a bathroom hook in Trey's studio?

"Honest, Lucy. Just talk," Trey was saying on the other side of the door.

Only it wasn't Trey talking, Lucy realized now. It was Mike. Mike. She couldn't believe it. That lying, deceitful bastard. How could he have done it? Mike, of all people. She'd trusted and believed in him. She'd stayed true to him, rejecting a love affair with a virile, extremely sexy "other man." Only there was no other man. Lucy was so wrapped up in righteous indignation at her ex-husband's duplicity, she conveniently forgot about her own.

"Lucy, don't scare me like this. If you don't open the door this instant, I'm going to—"

The door swung open. "What are you going to do, Trey?" she murmured with a come-hither smile as she stood there posing seductively in her white teddy, the damaging evidence once again neatly hung on the back of the bathroom door.

Mike was completely taken aback by the abrupt change in Lucy's demeanor. He regarded her suspiciously. "Are you . . . okay?"

She smiled seductively. "No. But I will be, soon." She stepped closer to him. "It can't be soon enough for me, Trey," she drawled.

His expression grew more wary. "I don't understand, Lucy. Just a couple of minutes ago—"

"I know. But I did it, Trey."

"Did it? Did what?"

"Exorcised him."

"Exorcised who?"

She trilled a little laugh. "Mike, silly. Stodgy, dull-as-a-dishcloth Mike. I guess somewhere in the back of my mind I still clung to the belief that I must have loved him to have married him."

Mike's stomach muscles twisted. "I'm sure you were in love with him, Lucy."

"Are you? Well, I'm not. I guess being with you this past week, Trey, has forced me to face some cold, hard truths." She slipped her arms around his neck, pleased as punch to feel him stiffen.

"What cold, hard truths?"

She nuzzled her face into the crook of his neck. "Put your arms around me, Trey. I'm so crazy about you, my knees are all wobbly."

Mike didn't budge. "What cold, hard truths, Lucy?" he demanded.

"You're so different from your brother, Trey. You're so much fun to be with."

"Are you saying you never had fun with Mike?"

Lucy smiled, her face hidden from him. She'd gotten him so upset he'd forgotten to alter the timbre of his voice.

"Oh, we had some . . . pleasant times, but it wasn't what I'd call fun," Lucy said airily. "Mike considered fun a waste of time and money."

"Aren't you being awfully hard on the guy, Lucy?"

She stroked his bare back. "You feel the same way about him, Trey. You've told me often enough."

"I know. But I wasn't . . . married to him."

Tantalizingly, she slipped her hand between them and lowered the zipper of his jeans. "Count yourself lucky, darling."

"Really, Lucy . . ."

"Oh, Trey. I'm so hot. I'm burning up with desire."

"Two minutes ago you said we were moving too fast." His jeans dropped around his ankles.

"That was two minutes ago. Too long, long minutes ago." She slipped one strap of her teddy off her shoulder. Then the other.

"Lucy." Mike backed away, shocked and appalled. Here was the woman he had loved to distraction tossing him aside like a wet dishrag and going after "his brother" like a bull-dozer.

"If only I could have met you first, Trey. Think of all the time we wasted."

As he bent to pull his jeans back up, Lucy threw herself, fireman-fashion, over his shoulder. "Carry me off, Trey. Make wild, passionate love to me like I should be made love to. Like I never was with Mike. I've always dreamed of one day finding a real man."

Okay. Now Mike was ripping mad. So he wasn't a real man. So he was a lousy lover. So she'd never even been in love with him. This whole ridiculous masquerade was for nothing. No—not nothing. He'd found out the truth. He'd learned Lucy's real feelings about him. Rage and devastation tore through him as he caught hold of his waistband, pulling his jeans back up as he straightened, lifting Lucy—who was still draped over his shoulder—with him.

He deposited her unceremoniously on the bed.

"Trey. You're so rough," Lucy cooed. "Someday you'll have to give your big brother pointers."

"From what he tells me," Mike lied unconvincingly, "your sister, Ellen, doesn't think he needs any pointers. He says she has absolutely no complaints."

"Really?" Lucy queried dubiously.

"You're damn straight," Mike snapped, grabbing up his shirt.

"Trey, darling, what are you doing? Is something wrong?" For all her desire to get back at Mike, she was starting to feel as if she might have gone too far. It was also at this point that she reminded herself she'd been equally duplicitous.

However furious and humiliated Mike felt, he wasn't about to let Lucy pull his cover now. He managed to get himself under control, and gave her a cool, distant look. "Sorry, baby. I just remembered I have a piece of business I didn't take care of. Why don't you just sit tight and keep the bed warm for me?"

Lucy knew he wasn't coming back. Just as she knew that if she let him walk out that door without telling him the truth—the whole truth—they might never manage to mend the fences.

Mike was at the door. His hand was on the knob. He was turning it.

Her mouth opened, but nothing came out. If she told him she knew his true identity, she'd have to also confess the truth about "Ellen."

He was stepping out the door. Only after he'd closed it behind him, did she call out weakly, "Mike."

MIKE FELT SICK TO HIS stomach as he stepped out of the renovated warehouse. He leaned against the wall of the building, sweat pouring from him. He shut his eyes, tears burning behind them. How could he have been so wrong about Lucy? Maybe, he thought, he was wrong about other things, as well. Namely, Lucy's sister, Ellen.

Unlike Lucy, Ellen appreciated him, wanted him, practically thought he was God's gift to women. He'd been so caught up in wooing Lucy back, he hadn't really given poor, well-meaning Ellen a fair chance. Or himself.

He started for the motorcycle, but stopped dead in his tracks. The masquerade and everything that went with it was over. He caught a cab and went home.

It took him a good hour to change himself back into "Clark Kent." On his way out of the bathroom he deposited his hairpiece in the wastebasket. As for "Trey's" ridiculous and outrageously expensive wardrobe, he'd donate every item to a worthwhile charity. He was standing by the mirror over his bureau combing his hair when he spotted a lone key resting in a small dish. The key to Ellen's apartment. The one she'd given him. The one he'd never used. He looked straight at his reflection.

"Face it, Mikey. You were an utter flop with Lucy, but maybe you can do better with her sister. What do you have to lose?" Silently, came the answer. *Nothing. I've already lost everything I really wanted.*

AFTER LUCY GOT DRESSED, she phoned Stephie. The baby-sitter told her she'd gone to a movie with her husband. Lucy didn't leave a message. Giving the paintings scattered around the studio a brief look, she wondered who had really painted them. Probably someone who knew someone who knew Uncle Paulie. She was sure Mike's uncle had had a hand in transforming Mike into Trey. As mad as she still was, she had to admit he'd done one hell of a job. Maybe she ought to drop in at the club and congratulate him.

WHEN MIKE GOT TO ELLEN'S apartment, he began to question his motives for going there. Did he really have feelings for Lucy's sister or was he using her to get back at his ex-wife? He told himself that Ellen was more his type. They thought alike, had the same values, the same interests. In fact, there was nothing they disagreed on. He envisioned the two of them going through life together without ever having a single argument. Ellen would never throw a plate of scrambled eggs at him, or anything else. She would always be reasonable, practical, sensible. Life with Ellen would be easygoing, placid and . . . impossibly, intolerably boring.

He stood outside her door. No, he wasn't being fair. Besides, Ellen wasn't as totally predictable as he'd thought. Visions of her in that frilly white apron emblazoned with the

phrase, We're Cooking Now, danced before his eyes. Maybe
he was underestimating life with Ellen. Maybe there were
more surprises in store for him than he realized!

He rang her bell. When she didn't answer, he realized that
he was truly disappointed. His hand slipped into his pocket.
She had given him the key. Chances were, she would be back
soon. What if he went inside and waited for her? Surprised
her? Maybe she still had that frilly apron tucked away. He
might suggest she try it on for him again....

He slipped the key in the lock and stepped inside the dark
apartment. Even before he flicked on the light, something
struck him as odd. It was the scent in the room. A familiar
scent. Not Ellen's—Lucy's. Lucy wore a very distinctive perfume. It was a scintillating blend of fruitiness and exotic
flowers. She'd been wearing it tonight at the studio. Had she
stopped in here to visit Ellen before heading over to his place?
Not "his" place, he reminded himself. "Trey" no longer existed. He would disappear forever. And good riddance to
him!

Mike resolved to let Lucy stew for a while—wondering
what had become of his sexy kid brother—and then tell her
the truth. He tried to soothe himself by imagining the delight
he would take in watching her face when she learned that
he—the man she'd scorned, belittled, humiliated—was none
other than the same man she'd tried so mightily to seduce.

He sighed, knowing already that there would be no delight
in it. He wondered if he'd take delight in anything ever again.

He flicked on the light. Unlike last night when the "flat" as
Ellen called it, had been as neat as a pin, now there were
clothes scattered about, a glass leaving a ring on the coffee
table, several magazines—fashion ones, at that—on the floor.
Mike frowned. That wasn't like Ellen at all.

Was she ill? Was that why she hadn't answered the door? He had a sick vision of her lying prone and lifeless on her bed. *Oh, God*, he thought. What if she'd felt so rejected when he'd run out on her last night that she'd—

"Ellen," he called out in a panic as he raced across the living room to the closed bedroom door. He flung it open.

She wasn't lying prone on the bed. She wasn't there. He felt a wave of exquisite relief, and vowed he would make it up to her somehow. But just as he was about to leave the room, something that *was* stretched out across the bed caught his eye. Something familiar.

Slowly, he walked over to the bed and picked up the bathrobe. There on the rolled collar was the all-too-familiar monogram, L.W.P. Lucy Warner Powell. Caught on the back of the collar were some strands of hair. Lucy's blond strands mingled with "Ellen's" brown ones.

He wandered into the bathroom and found just what he now expected he would find—a bottle of brown hair rinse. He sat down on the edge of the tub and stared at it. Why, that lying, conniving, deceitful, low-down . . .

She'd played him for a complete fool every which way. A deep scowl etched his features. She must be having herself quite a laugh at his expense, right about now.

"Come on, Lucy. Will you stop looking so glum?" Uncle Paulie cajoled. "You're gonna drive away all my customers."

"Why'd you do it? Why'd Mike do it?"

"Why? Because he's nuts about you. And I'm nuts about both of you. You two belong together. What's better to hold on to, kid? A grudge or the man of your dreams?"

"I said some awful things about him. I was so mad. And you know how I get when I get mad, Uncle Paulie."

"Hey, you're making progress. You didn't throw anything at him, right?"

"Maybe it's true what they say about sticks and stones breaking your bones but words never harming you. But the heart isn't a bone. Words can do a lot more harm to that fragile muscle than a piece of bone china."

Uncle Paulie placed a hand over that of his teary ex-niece-in-law. "Take an old, experienced bartender's advice. Go home, Lucy. Call Mike up. Tell him to hightail it back home so the two of you can hash it all out."

"I can't," Lucy said forlornly. No more than she could bring herself to admit to Uncle Paulie that she'd played the same rotten, underhanded trick on Mike that he'd played on her. The truth just stuck in her throat like a chicken bone.

On her way home Lucy had an idea—one that she thought just might work. She asked the cabbie to take her to "Ellen's" flat rather than back to the Harkness Towers. Once she got there, she would transform herself into her sister and then call up Mike and beg him to come over.

Maybe she couldn't just come right out and admit the truth, but once "Ellen" put Mike in a more forgiving frame of mind, she might have the courage to finally reveal the truth. The whole truth.

MIKE WAS STILL SITTING on the edge of the bathtub trying to absorb all the ramifications of the discovery he'd just made when he heard the front door opening. Ellen. No, not Ellen. There *was* no Ellen. That left only one other possibility. Lucy. His duplicitous ex-wife returning to "the scene of the crime"!

Dashing into the bedroom, Mike dove under the bed just as Lucy stepped in. Any remaining doubts about the new arrival were immediately squelched when two turquoise-blue pumps walked past him. He heard the sound of a zipper opening. An instant later, a familiar turquoise-blue trifle of a dress dropped to the floor a few inches from Mike's nose. For all his anger, he couldn't help remembering how incredible Lucy had looked in that dress. Nor could he keep from remembering how she looked without it.

The mattress and box spring dipped as Lucy sat down on the edge of her bed. He pictured her in that white lace teddy. . . .

For a few moments there was absolute silence, then he heard Lucy dialing the phone. Who was she calling? Trey? Ha!

But it wasn't Trey.

"Hello, Mike. It's Ellen. Would you give me a call as soon as you get home, love? Better still, come straight over. I must talk to you. It's an . . . emergency."

The phone clicked. Under the bed, Mike steamed. How could he not have seen through that laid-on British accent? How could he have been so gullible as to believe Lucy really had a twin sister? And one, no less, who was the exact opposite of her. His anger welled. Sure, he'd done the same thing, but his motives were honorable. He'd wanted to prove to Lucy that he could be the kind of man she wanted. Even if, along the way, he'd discovered that he really couldn't be. Didn't want to be. He needed Lucy to love him for who he was. Ha-ha.

As for Lucy's little charade, he didn't attribute her with any such honorable intentions. After what she had told "Trey" about her true feelings, Mike was convinced Lucy had just been having a little fun at his expense. More than likely, she'd invited him over tonight to have her last laugh.

He was so deep in thought it took him a minute or two to realize Lucy had left the bedroom. He heard the shower running. A smile slowly curled his lips as he felt in his pocket for the brown hair rinse he'd absently stuck there. No doubt, she'd be looking all over for it. How could she be "Ellen" without the brown hair?

LUCY SCOWLED. WHERE was the hair rinse? Squinting from the water in her eyes, she stuck her head out of the shower to see if she'd left it on the bathroom sink. It wasn't there. But she did spot it an instant later. In Mike's hand. He was standing at the open bathroom door, holding it out to her.

"Really, Lucy. You should thank your lucky stars you're a natural blonde. Brown hair just doesn't become you. But then, some sacrifices are worth it, I suppose."

Lucy stood there, clutching the shower curtain to her body, dumbfounded.

He looked at the bottle, smiled derisively, then dropped it in the wastebasket.

"You won't be needing it anymore," he said soberly, then turned and walked out of the room.

"Mike!" Lucy called out. Dripping wet and naked, she stepped out of the shower and rushed out of the bathroom. But by the time she made it to the living room, Mike was exiting the front door.

"Mike. Wait!" she called out again.

He turned for an instant, his expression blank. "You'd better put something on, Lucy." He started out the door, but then turned back to her one more time. "Come to think of it, you and Trey are a perfect match."

"You're right," she snapped angrily. "It's just too bad he doesn't exist."

Mike blinked several times. "What?"

"Did you really think I was that gullible?" Lucy laughed sharply, and grabbed up a candy dish.

"Lucy. Now, Lucy..."

Mike made it out into the hall in the nick of time because the dish crashed against the door.

14

"YOU'RE CALLING ME deceitful? Of all the nerve..." Lucy sputtered.

"And I'll tell you something else," Mike countered. "'Ellen' was a complete bore."

"A bore? A bore?"

"You heard me. The way she went on endlessly about nothing. And those outfits. Give me a break. She could have won an award for Matron of the Year."

"And I suppose you think Trey was a real lady-killer just because he rode some dumb motorcycle and walked around in ridiculous undershirts."

"Those were not undershirts. They were high-fashion tank tops. La Férlia tank tops. And they cost a fortune."

"And those leather pants. Really, Mike. Who did you think you were? Marlon Brando?"

"What about those stupid glasses 'Ellen' wore? They made your nose really veer to the right."

EUNICE POURED CLARA a cup of tea as they sat at their table on the terrace. It was rather a bit brisk out, but until it got really cold they enjoyed taking their morning meal outdoors. Especially this morning.

"Isn't it nice that they're back together," Eunice said, buttering her English muffin.

Clara scowled. "Nice. Well, it certainly isn't nice the way they're talking about each other's siblings. If anyone spoke about my sister, Nancy, the way Mike Powell spoke to Lucy about her sister Ellen, I'd have punched him right in the jaw."

Eunice's eyes sparkled. "Or tossed a piece of china at him anyway."

"I will say that Lucy's right about that brother of Mike's, though," Clara conceded. "The minute I laid eyes on that wild, unkempt-looking man, I knew he wasn't to be trusted."

"Certainly the wrong man for Lucy," Eunice agreed. "And I can't picture Ellen and Mike together. Why, there'd be no sparks at all."

"YOU THINK YOU WERE so clever," Mike charged. "But you didn't pull one over on me."

"Liar," Lucy countered. "I saw through you long before you saw through me."

"Liar."

"Don't you dare call me a liar."

"Liar, liar, liar," Mike taunted.

"I'm warning you, Mike Powell...."

EUNICE AND CLARA WATCHED a plate whiz down past them.

"I do believe you were wrong about their china," Clara said nonchalantly. "It isn't Cynthia's pattern."

"You may be right, Clara," Eunice allowed, reaching for a second English muffin. "But it's quite similar."

Clara eyed the one English muffin left on the plate. She pursed her lips. Her attempts at dieting had not gone well at all.

Eunice observed her friend and smiled. "Oh, go on, Clara. Live a little. Throw caution to the winds."

Clara eyed the muffin, eyed her friend, and then her usually solemn mouth broke out into a broad grin. "Why not," she decided.

Instead of caution, however, it was the china dish that Clara Ponds threw to the winds. With a cavalier fling, she tossed it right over the balcony—after retrieving that last English muffin.

"Why, Clara!" Eunice giggled.

And then both women began to laugh in earnest.

"I DID WARN YOU," Lucy said, backing away as he advanced toward her.

"Is this ever going to stop?" Mike asked, his expression unreadable.

"I don't know," she admitted. "I do have a temper. You know that."

He advanced a few more steps. "I know."

"I . . . I can't change, Mike. I tried. I really did. But I can't be self-contained, sensible, practical. . . ."

"I know that, too."

She backed into the terrace wall. Mike kept coming until they were practically nose to nose. "I can't change, either, Lucy. I'll never be suave and freewheeling, throw money around like it was water . . ."

Her breath was coming in rapid little spurts. "I know."

"So, where does that leave us, Lucy?" As he posed the question, his fingers slid over the monogram on her bathrobe.

His light touch electrified her. "I'm not sure," she said, her voice reverberating with desire.

"You never did have the monogram changed. L.W.P. Lucy Warner Powell. I guess the *P's* pretty superfluous."

"Oh, I don't know," Lucy murmured.

"Don't you?" His fingers found their way to the tie of her robe. He tugged it loose so that it fell open. She was wearing a thin, silky, pale peach nightie. He grinned. "'Ellen' would rather have died than wear something like this, I bet."

Lucy grinned back, shrugging out of her robe. "Definitely."

She began unbuttoning his preppy button-down oxford shirt. "And 'Trey' wouldn't be caught dead in something like this."

"You're so right," he said, shrugging it off.

"What? No La Ferlia tank top?" she quipped as she ran her fingers lightly down his bare chest.

"You mean an overpriced undershirt. No way."

Delicately, he lowered one strap of her nightie. In the bright morning light, he could detect a faint hint of that purple birthmark that had been the finishing touch in convincing him Lucy was Ellen. He kissed the spot.

Lucy moaned softly, her body swaying involuntarily. "Shouldn't we . . . go inside?"

He lifted his head and leveled his gaze on her, his expression solemn. "Not until we settle something first."

It couldn't be settled fast enough to suit Lucy. Never had she wanted Mike more.

"Settle . . . what?"

He took firm hold of her bare shoulders, the other strap of her nightie having slipped off. "Just this. I love you, Lucy Warner Powell. Just the way you are."

Tears spilled over Lucy's lids. "Oh, and I love you, Michael Lloyd Powell. Just the way you are."

"We'll get into fights every day, you know."

"But what fun we'll have," Lucy murmured, "making up every night."

"It isn't nighttime yet," he said huskily as she took hold of the waistband of his trousers and began to tug him inside the apartment.

"Can you handle it?"

"Can I handle it?" Before she knew what was happening, he had scooped her up in his arms. "I'll give it my best."

Lucy pressed her cheek against his bare shoulder. "What more could a woman ask for?"

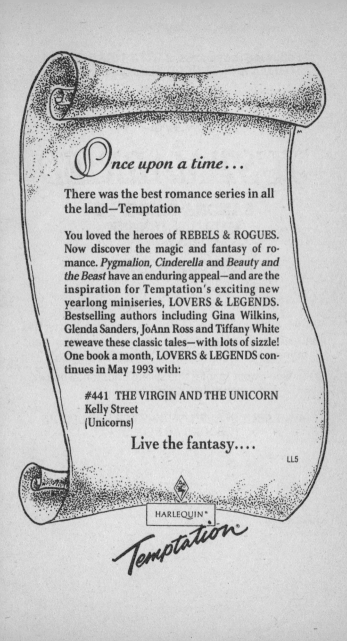

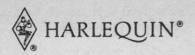

HARLEQUIN®

THE TAGGARTS OF TEXAS!

Harlequin's Ruth Jean Dale brings you
THE TAGGARTS OF TEXAS!

Those Taggart men—strong, sexy and hard to resist...

You've met Jesse James Taggart in FIREWORKS!
Harlequin Romance #3205 (July 1992)

And Trey Smith—he's THE RED-BLOODED YANKEE!
Harlequin Temptation #413 (October 1992)

And the unforgettable Daniel Boone Taggart in SHOWDOWN!
Harlequin Romance #3242 (January 1993)

Now meet Boone Smith and the Taggarts who started it all—
in LEGEND!
Harlequin Historical #168 (April 1993)

Read all the Taggart romances!
Meet all the Taggart men!

Available wherever Harlequin Books are sold.

Where do you find hot Texas nights, smooth Texas charm and dangerously sexy cowboys?

Crystal Creek

AMARILLO BY MORNING

Show time—Texas style!

Everybody loves a cowboy, and Cal McKinney is one of the best. So when designer Serena Davis approaches this handsome rodeo star, the last thing Cal expects is a business proposition!

CRYSTAL CREEK reverberates with the exciting rhythm of Texas. Each story features the rugged individuals who live and love in the Lone Star State. And each one ends with the same invitation...

Y'ALL COME BACK...REAL SOON!

Don't miss *AMARILLO BY MORNING* by Bethany Campbell. Available in May wherever Harlequin books are sold.

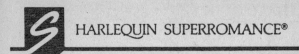

HARLEQUIN SUPERROMANCE®

HARLEQUIN SUPERROMANCE NOVELS WANTS TO INTRODUCE YOU TO A DARING NEW CONCEPT IN ROMANCE...

WOMEN WHO DARE!
Bright, bold, beautiful...
Brave and caring, strong and passionate...
They're women who know their own minds
and will dare anything...
for love!

One title per month in 1993, written by popular Superromance authors, will highlight our special heroines as they face unusual, challenging and sometimes dangerous situations.

Next month, time and love collide in:
#549 PARADOX by Lynn Erickson
Available in May wherever Harlequin Superromance novels are sold.

HARLEQUIN ✦ PRESENTS®

A Year
DOWN UNDER

In 1993, Harlequin Presents celebrates the land down under. In May, let us take you to Auckland, New Zealand, in SECRET ADMIRER by Susan Napier, Harlequin Presents #1554.

Scott Gregory is ready to make his move. He's realized Grace is a novice at business *and* emotionally vulnerable—a young widow struggling to save her late husband's company. But Grace is a fighter. She's taking business courses and she's determined not to forget Scott's reputation as a womanizer. Even if it means adding another battle to the war—a fight against her growing attraction to the handsome New Zealander!

Share the adventure—and the romance—
of A Year Down Under!

Available this month in
A YEAR DOWN UNDER

A DANGEROUS LOVER
by Lindsay Armstrong
Harlequin Presents #1546
Wherever Harlequin books are sold.

YDU-A